NURSERY SCHOOL

G.D.GREY

THIS EDITION
COPYRIGHT©
G.D.GREY
2017
ISBN: 9781976879258
Imprint: Independently published

Front and rear cover designs © Charlie Fox

ALL RIGHTS RESERVED

FOREWORD

This is the first volume of a series concerning the adventures of Alice Darwin and her friend Rachel Katz. Their parents are, respectively, market gardeners and physicians; they are also agents of Her Majesty's Government. The girls were born within two days of each other in the same country hospital which is how their two mothers met for the first time. This chance meeting created a lifetime friendship between the two sets of parents and enabled their children to thrive in an atmosphere of intelligent tolerance and understanding of their essential natures. Surrounded by woodlands, forest animals and the protection and love of their elders, they developed martial art skills and survival tactics quite unusual for English children. As they are home taught by extremely tough and knowledgeable people, their education is far in advance of their contemporaries. They also have enough intelligence and innate good nature to mix happily with their peers when they finally enter secondary school. Their parents have been careful to ensure that they are also very civilised human beings in spite of the fact that most of their time is either spent in combat sports with each other or absorbing book knowledge at a prodigious rate. In spite of this they remain fiercely independent and self-reliant which stands them in good stead on any number of their hair-raising escapades. They also have a fine sense of humour which sustains them through some difficult times later in life. Accounts of their later adventures can be found in the Finishing School series which are available from Amazon self-publishing in either paperback or as an ebook.

NURSERY SCHOOL

CHAPTER I

Alice Darwin and Rachel Katz were born within two days of each other in the same local maternity ward of the cottage hospital at Milford St Evelyn in the county of Devonshire (North). The cottage hospital had only one maternity ward, one accident and emergency ward and a pharmacy. It had served the local community well for over a hundred years, but 1964, when our story begins, was almost its last year in existence before the heavy and interfering hand of Whitehall brought about its dissolution together with the similar fate of other small and well-loved institutions which were suddenly crowded together in large urban centres and would involve the inhabitants of outlying villages and small towns very often having to travel long distances to get the help and attention they needed. Ecologically, economically and culturally these moves to centralise facilities in already busy urban areas have not proved to be a very great success. The only real beneficiaries are the politicos and Whitehall mandarins whose egos have had a pleasant and stimulating massage. For the rest of the population it has been little short of a disaster, but the English are so used to their political masters doing little else but satisfy their own need for self-aggrandisement that they have resignedly accepted the shortage of any particular sense of intelligent use of their resources. Middle management has gained a stranglehold on the nation and the driving force of all social forces is in the hands of accountants, soothsayers and marketing personnel. So much for the state of the nation and back to our two young ladies who, in the days which I opened this chronicle had just entered the world and were to play a not insignificant rôle in the security and health of the country in their later years,

Their mothers, Vera Darwin and Rebecca Katz, could not have been a more disparate couple. Vera Darwin, small and feisty with ruddy complexion and hair which gave the impression of blackened steel wool, and Rebecca Katz, kindly, soft spoken and every inch the epitome of Jewish motherhood, had met at what passed for the prenatal class run by the hospital and organised so that a medical check-up was taken at necessary intervals. This was always positive as both mothers were very conscious of the need to be as healthy as possible for the arrival of the new addition to their families. Consequently they both ate well, exercised within reason, rested a lot and listened to hypnotic recordings of guided meditations and sounds of whales singing and birds tweeting! What finally cemented their friendship was the birth of a baby girl to Rebecca who, when the nurse tried to take the baby away from her as was the custom in those days, was gently rebuked by the mother who refused to part with her newborn. Fortunately Matron, generally acknowledged as the gaoler from Cell Block H, was not there to back up the trainee nurse who was trying to separate the two. Vera Darwin, propped up in the neighbouring bed, remarking that obviously the trainee nurse had never witnessed an attempt to separate a tiger cub from its mother, otherwise she would not have put herself into such mortal peril, persuaded the young nurse that discretion was the better part of valour. She reluctantly withdrew from her attempt, merely muttering that Matron would have something to say about this when she came back from sick leave. This did not happen until Vera herself had just been delivered of her own baby girl. A feeble and vain attempt was made by the trainee nurse to extract the new arrival from where she was lying on her mother's breast. The nurse petitioned Matron for support and Matron came bustling into the ward full of righteous indignation, hospital rules and procedures bursting from every pore and made to put her hands on the infant. Vera sat up further in the bed and addressed Matron thus;

"If you lay one finger on either myself or my baby I shall have you up for assault. My husband is an eminent lawyer and is only too happy when acting for the prosecution in cases such as this. I can't tell you the number of successes he has had. Furthermore, if you do manage to get your hands where they should not be, I shall pass my newborn over to my good friend, Mrs. Katz. She will guard my child while you and I go out into the car-park and settle this once and for all. Do you understand?"

"Doctor will have to be told," was Matron's flushed and nervous response. At that moment Doctor himself walked into the ward to inspect his patients. Matron voluble, Doctor ingratiating. Vera stared at them stonily. Rebecca swung her legs out of the bed and sat up with baby Rachel at her breast and supported the new mother by staring stonily at them as well. Matron withdrew. Doctor withdrew. Nurse went to put the kettle on, the two new mothers smiled complicitly at each other and peace returned to the ward.

"I thought your husband was a market gardener," Rebecca said.

"So he is, but these idiots don't know that, do they!"

Another factor which brought them together, apart from their mutual ambitions for good parenting, was a secret, unknown to either of them at the time, of their clandestine careers. Both ladies, in fact, worked as agents of the British Government. Their public personas and professions and that of their husbands were as follows: Vera Darwin and her husband Tom, ran a garden centre and would from time to time disappear into a jungle somewhere in search of a rare plant for research purposes. This would usually coincide with a local upheaval or destabilisation being carried out by a power foreign to the country concerned in order to exploit its natural resources. (More often than not the CIA were just that foreign power destabilising away like there was no tomorrow and much to the annoyance of HM's own concerns which had to try to keep smiling in the face of whatever antics the Americans were up to). The same situation faced Rebecca and her husband Joseph, both good people and medical researchers who would go abroad for periods to work with *Medicins sans frontiéres* and similar institutions in places where, owing to British Arms manufacturers and other companies who should have known better, local tribesmen were being furnished with horrific weaponry with which they were enabled to gleefully terrorise a whole country.

Tom and Vera owned a smallholding surrounded by farmland on the south western edge of the village and Rebecca and Joseph had the Old Vicarage at the other end of Milford St. Evelyn which accounted for the fact of their not having met before in spite of being beholden to the same employer. By the time the babies arrived both families had come to be on visiting terms and the new additions to the couples cemented the growing friendship between the four of them. Each couple was, by nature of their employment and also on account of personal inclination, inclined to a certain reluctance to make new friends, but the as yet undisclosed nature of the clandestine aspects of their occupations was slowly but surely establishing a natural bonding. There were also practical benefits to be had from baby minding and freeing each couple for an evening at least for a trip to the cinema or a night out at the local pub or sometimes a day to visit Taunton or Bristol for a shopping spree. They were eventually let into each others' secret lives by their masters in MI6 who, with full knowledge of their situation, explained to each couple the circumstances of their new friends' private lives. The purpose of this was to reassure both couples that, although they had been free to take time off for the birth of their respective daughters, nevertheless it would be appreciated if they would continue with the valuable service they had willingly signed up for prior to their parenthood.

  The plan was that each couple would take it in turn to accept an assignment and the other couple would parent their child. As both couples had indeed become so easily accepting and trusting of each other, this was given some serious consideration. Another factor which boded quite hopefully for the arrangement was that when both babies had got to the crawling stage they had seemingly bonded in eternal friendship and were never happier than when they were together. This is not to say that they sat with each other in amiable chortling play, quite the reverse in fact. There was a distinct tendency for them to grapple and make primitive attempts to eviscerate each other in the most bloodthirsty way. Any attempt to separate them, however, was met with strenuous protestation and the undeniable fact was that they never appeared to have caused each other any serious damage whatsoever.

  Joseph, being a quiet and thoughtful person, carefully observed them at play and in his opinion they were perfectly healthy young animals whose game playing was developmental in the same way as any other young animals, especially of the feline species.

"Are you saying, Joseph," demanded Vera truculently, "that our babies, our dear little children are no more than cats, tom-cats at that?"

"More or less, Vera," Joseph agreed placidly. "You see, young animals learn how to defend themselves in their play. They don't hurt each other because they are bonded, either by blood or tribal cohesion, to protect themselves and other members of their family or tribe and Alice and Rachel are doing just that, so I would suggest you just let them get on with it. Nature takes care of things in her own way. She's been around much longer than any of us and the wise person doesn't interfere with their nature or anybody else's nature either if they've got any sense."

"Well, that puts the Holy Roman Church in it's place, doesn't it!" said Tom amusedly.

"Please let us not talk of such horrors in front of the children," Joseph said, giving a fond glance at the two little creatures rough-housing away on the floor. Suddenly they both stopped and looked up at the adults grouped around them. They both started giggling at the same time and their mothers picked them up for a kiss and cuddle before they were taken for the ritual nappy change and afternoon rest, which was usually taken in a sling round whichever parents neck happened to be available.

"Do you think they're going to be lifelong friends?" Tom asked Joseph somewhat wistfully as he nursed both babies in his arms.

"I wouldn't be surprised," he replied. "It might be a bit difficult in later life for them, what with us being a bit solitary and bringing them up the way we have to. They'll most likely build up a mutual reliance which, if it matures and remains constant will be a wondrous force in their lives. Very few of us have that sort of deep friendship which is a sad reflection on this every man for himself culture which seems to have taken root in our society."

"Damon and Pythias spring to mind of course," Tom said. "But nowadays little is known about the classical forms of love. The only kind most people acknowledge nowadays is erotic and anything else is suspect and food and drink for the gutter press."

"Oh, I think most people experience *agape* and *storge* somewhat more readily than *eros* in spite of the News of the World, you know."

"Add *phileo* to that and maybe you are right. I confess to a certain cynicism with regard to the modern age, but in reality it's probably a darned sight better than some previous times. There is a bit more kindness around nowadays, in England at least. Certainly better than just after the end of the war. So much fear and bitterness under the surface. Only to be expected after all that turmoil."

"I think you must have witnessed some unpleasant things, Tom," Joseph said sympathetically. Tom grunted.

"I got called up in 1943 and went for the RAF, but they shoved me into the SIS and that's the way I got through the war and I'm not allowed to talk about any of it which is perhaps just as well. Anyway, our masters have now told us of their plans for us. What do you think of them, Joe?"

"Our masters or their plans?"

"One surely does not speak of them in the same breath!" Tom said, adding, "Not if one wants to remain indifferent to political pressure while keeping a purely professional approach to our work."

"I think that the idea is sensible and obviously in all our best interests. I just hope that our assignments are short enough so that the girls remember who their birth parents are when we come home. But perhaps that won't matter quite so much if they have the security of one set of parents and each other. They might even begin to view us as interchangeable suppliers of their needs except when they want to play one of us off against the other. Young animals are notoriously unscrupulous especially young human animals."

"How true," Rebecca said, having just experienced a particularly hair-raising bath-time. "They were being extraordinarily bad mannered this evening. Do you think they know something about our plans for the future?"

"I wouldn't be at all surprised," Tom said. "How is it that the dogs always know what's going on almost before we know it ourselves? Look at the way they were waiting at the door the other day; five whole minutes before our anonymous messenger arrived. The fur was up on both their backs."

"Yes, I must say that I didn't take very kindly to that young man," said Joseph. "Full of his own importance and ruffled feathers because he thought himself above such a mundane task as delivering communications from head office."

"Full of bullshit, more like," Tom growled. "Probably nervous of the countryside, mind. Needs lots of concrete to walk on to feel safe."

"Never mind all that," Vera had come into the kitchen. Joseph, Rebecca and Rachel were staying at Tom and Vera's house over the weekend so that they could plan ahead for the forthcoming absence of the Darwins which was to start in three weeks time when they would get on a plane to South America. Once arrived they would then be given further instructions and would probably be unreachable for the ensuing two months. It would be a long time in their child's life and Vera was naturally fearful of the effect it might have on her relationship with her daughter.

"I think we should begin to get Alice used to staying overnight with you and see how that works out. If she's not entirely happy about the situation then we will not be doing this."

"Good for you, my dear," Rebecca was supportive as always. "We'll see how it goes, but I think you will find that it will just be a nice adventure for her. I hope so anyway. If she gets distressed of course I'll ring you immediately."

The next morning the Katzs drove back to the Old Vicarage with both babies. Neither of them was completely weaned, so the separation was also a test to see how Alice got on with Rebecca as surrogate wet nurse and how Rebecca got on supplying enough for the needs of both babies. Both mothers had tried this out with what had been intended as a short feed, first from Vera, lying propped up in bed with a baby at each breast, and then with Rebecca taking over halfway through. The result had surprised both mothers as their two offspring had happily accepted each surrogate breast with enthusiasm.

"I do hope this is not going to encourage them to accept drinks from strangers when they get older," Vera said plaintively.

"Don't worry, my dear," Rebecca replied. "I expect they'll turn out very well. Look at the little darlings. They're so sweet when they're either at the breast or fast asleep, aren't they."

"Indeed so," snapped Vera. "It's only all the other times when hell breaks loose."

CHAPTER II

When Vera and Tom returned to England some three months later it was a late Autumn of 1965. October was quite warm and sunny that year following some erratic temperatures the preceding months. The little girls were now staggering about on tottery legs and babbling to each other in some language of their own which was totally incomprehensible to the rest of the household. Rebecca was relieved that both babies had started on solids and only very occasionally demanded her milk, which was probably just as well as Vera's milk supply had dried up finally by the time they reached Caracas. The prodigal parents were met at the airport by Joseph who drove them home.

"We were officially debriefed on the plane back," Tom explained to Joseph. "I expect we'll have another meeting soon for more corroborative details as to whether we're still secure or not. I think it went all right, but you're never entirely sure whether or not some little detail will fall into place in the minds of locals to make them suspicious."

"As you very well know," Vera added.

"I agree. It's getting perilously close to exposure for us as well. Fortunately not a whisper of betrayal or suspicion as yet, but if our faces show up once too often in the wrong place, life is going to get more fraught than usual and it's fraught enough as it is."

"I just pray that it never follows us back home," Tom said grimly. "We've got more to lose now with our offspring. Perhaps we should chuck it in before it gets critical. Hell, we've been doing this for how many years?"

"We were conscripted over ten years ago," Joseph said, "I think we've done fifteen missions to date."

"Quite enough for one's country I would have thought," Vera said. "Every time we come back I swear it will be the last time and here we are still running around at their beck and call like fucking sheep dogs, and I reckon that's about the extent of their consideration for us."

Tom took her hand in his. "We would be bored out of our minds if we didn't do this at least twice a year," he said. "Don't take any notice, Joseph, this is just part of the unwinding process. Give her another couple of months and she'll be getting antsy again and raring to dive into the danger zone once more. That goes for me too. I'm quite happy to leave the garden centre in Jerry's hands. He's very capable and as he closely resembles me, most people don't notice the difference so nobody asks too many awkward questions. And it's OK for you and Rebecca as well as everybody is used to you going off to conferences on advances in medicine and medical jurisprudence, not to mention *Medicins sans frontieres* etcetera."

"Kind of you to say so," Joseph replied, skilfully overtaking an overburdened lorry. "I always think it's safer to be in front of those things in case their load sheds itself under our wheels."

"Just so," commented Vera. "And make sure you're well ahead of them in case they go to sleep at the wheel and tear into the back of the car. Please remember that we are here in the back seats."

"As if I would be likely to overlook that fact, in consideration of the continuous advice I am receiving concerning my considerable driving skills, informed as they are by at least twenty years of first hand experience and a certificate from the Advanced School of Motoring and the Police Academy at Hendon."

"That would be the Advanced School of Motoring, Azerbaijan, would it? And the Police Academy in Hendon, Tanganyika, yes?"

"Perfectly correct, dear lady," Joseph replied, smoothly. He overtook a line of slow-moving cars.

"If I don't survive this journey will you please make sure that Rebecca takes care of our child and that she is, under pain of condign punishment, never to travel in any vehicle being driven by her husband."

Tom gave her hand a squeeze and kissed her gently. "Of course, my love. And you shall have fresh flowers placed on your grave every Sunday and a Mass said for your soul on Saints' days."

"Thank you, Tom. That is a sweet thought. Did you hear that, Joseph?"

****

They arrived at their home in time for tea. Joseph and Rebecca had divided their time between the two houses. The two bull-terriers, which belonged to the Darwins, were quite happy in either house as were the two toddlers, but naturally it was better that the travellers should come home to a warm, lived-in house rather than a cold and empty one. The Aga had been kept going during their absence so the place was warm, dry and welcoming. The little girls were out playing in the garden. Alice had Rachel by the hair and was dragging her towards the pond near the fenced off paddock which had a couple of horses grazing. Alice let go of

Rachel's hair when Rebecca called out to them that tea was ready and that they had visitors. Rachel, seemingly untroubled, staggered after her tormentor and tackled her, rugby fashion. Alice rolled over and punched her in the face and Rachel retaliated by climbing on top and pinning her to the ground. Rebecca hoicked Rachel up and tucking her under one arm used her other arm to gather up Alice, still flailing about with both arms and legs. She carried the two into the kitchen and plonked them down in their high-chairs. She waggled an admonitory finger.

"Peace," she commanded, "or no tea. And no visitors." Both children suddenly became model citizens and beamed on the assembled company. Alice threw her arms open and Vera plucked her out of the chair to give her a resounding kiss.

"Christ, you're a weight!" were her first words to her daughter, who giggled. She handed her over to her husband who kissed her and did fatherly things like throwing her into the air, catching her and swinging her up and down. Then Vera picked Rachel up and gave her a kiss and a hug and exclaimed, 'Well, you are no lightweight either. What have they been feeding you? Concrete chip cookies with iron filings sprinkle? My, but you are both big girls aren't you. Are you still feeding them?" she asked her friend. Rebecca told her that it was only occasionally now, to which Vera replied that it was just as well as she had dried up completely and she didn't fancy having to revive her milk production even if that were possible. Rebecca said not to worry as she was content to continue being Earth Mother if needed.

"I think you rather enjoy it," Vera said, smilingly.

"I do that," Rebecca agreed. "It's one of the most lovely and satisfying moments to sit there with the two of them suckling away. I hope you don't feel neglected or anything," she regarded Vera with concern.

"Good Lord, no," said Vera firmly. "I don't feel as if I have missed something, nor do I feel jealous or bereft or anything. I'm just so happy that you were here to look after them both and give them what they needed." She put Rachel back in her chair and went over to Rebecca to give her a hug. "Hey, it's so good to see you both again and I am so happy to be back with you all. Hello doggies, You want some kisses too don't you, yes you do!"

She made a fuss of the two dogs who rolled around ecstatically and the two little girls joined in with a babble of incomprehensible chatter accompanied by throwing bits of their bread and butter slices at the animals.

"These are not good for the dogs," Joseph explained patiently to the pair. "But they are good for you. So good, in fact, that if you don't eat them, then you won't get any fruit cake because we will think you are not well and have to put you both in the duck-pond to cool off." This brought screams of merriment from the high-chairs but the occupants applied themselves diligently to their home-made baked bread.

"I've made a sort of hotpot and I thought we might share a bottle of wine tonight," Joseph said. Both he and Rebecca were excellent cooks, Rebecca's fruitcake renowned locally as an exemplar of all fruitcakes and Joseph's Pavlova and his sherry trifle gaining equivalent accolades.

"What a lovely idea. In the meantime a nice pot of tea would go down a treat with some of your fruitcake. We would then know we were back in civilisation." Vera and Tom went out to the car to fetch in their cases.

"No presents, I'm afraid. We had a rather hurried departure and what can one get at airports that we cannot get elsewhere? By the time you've lugged it all back it's not worth the effort. None of us smoke or drink - well, hardly at all - so there's no profit in that. Try to find a decent cup of tea south of Dover - you might as well hunt for the Holy Grail!"

Then came the turn of Rebecca and Joseph. Their destination was Rhodesia as Ian Smith was becoming increasingly intransigent about accepting the rise of power from the native population. At the same time the British Government was becoming nervous about the unilateralism of the Rhodesian Prime Minister and felt the need for first-hand reports on the strength of his local support. Gunboat diplomacy had rebounded badly on the Eden government in the previous decade and had considerably weakened the control and power of the British Empire. In effect it saw the end of the British Empire as the end had come to so many of the European Empires which had unravelled since the turn of the century.

CHAPTER III

A couple of years later saw our two little people enrolled in nursery school. Of course they were somewhat larger little people by then, and thanks to their excellent diet of unadulterated milk and dairy produce, and in spite of their absolute refusal of meat or fowl, they were both sturdy and, owing to their adventurous natures, agile and resilient to most childhood ailments. They were also strikingly similar in appearance to each other in these formative years. Their Uncle Jerry, Tom's brother, likened them to a female version of Tweedledum and Tweedledee, which was a not inaccurate description of them both, especially in those moments of rest after some particularly gruelling combat, when they would stand with their arms round each other's shoulders and contemplate the world with innocent smiling faces. To the other children in the nursery they were beacons of light and hope and to the two elderly sisters and their staff of one other younger woman, who had a confused notion of discipline and how to manage three-year-olds, they were a holy terror. It wasn't that they were in any way defiant of their guardians, but more that they treated the two good ladies and their helpmeet with a polite disdain and ran the sessions to their own wishes, overriding any commands which went against their plans for the games they were going to play on that day. Miss Eileen, the elder sister would, for instance, suggest a quiet morning in the schoolroom engaged in some fun with crayons and sheets of paper. This would usually occur when the weather was not very pleasant. There would be a cold wind blowing and maybe even the threat of some rain. Miss Eileen would hand out paper and crayons (non-poisonous, of course) to the children and they would all seem to settle down to draw pretty pictures. Miss Eileen would retreat behind a novel when they appeared to have settled down quietly to their artistic efforts. The next time she looked up from her book, the classroom would be empty and she would see Tweedledum, possibly Tweedledee, or both, organising a game of hopscotch or similar activity outside in the playground. All the children would be properly dressed in outdoor clothes, a process which normally would take a good ten minutes for all the twenty or so children who normally constituted the assembly, but in this case appeared to have been achieved in a record three minutes flat, only time enough for Miss Eileen to have got halfway down the second page of her Mills & Boon novelette before being dragged back to reality by the excited childish squeals coming through the window from the playground. She and her sister soon realised that to make any attempt to coax the children back into the warm classroom would only result in the sort of emotional upheaval which is very difficult to control and is also extremely wearing on the nerves of those who have caused it in the first place. The principal characters, who are all bawling their heads off, (with the exception, it is needless to say, of the two instigators of this unauthorised activity), are naturally having the time of their lives creating a wondrous Babel of hysteria which is doing no good to the interior well-being and equanimity of their oppressors. Consequently Miss Eileen and her sister Miss Felicity, eschewing protocol, allowed the holy terrors to run the show for them, all of which would have continued to work very well except for the Fly in the Ointment, Miss Carnegie. Now, Miss Carnegie was a perfectly decent young woman but one of so many who go into education with the bright ideas of transforming their charges into models of the perfect people that they had imagined they should themselves be. This invariably ends in tears of course, and in this particular case, ended up with Miss Carnegie leaving the teaching profession eventually for a better paid and older profession and one where she had much more control over the unfortunates in her care. I refer of course to the nursing profession and not one of the darker areas of an even older profession which you might have thought was being implied.

    Her downfall on the occasion I am about to relate, came as a result of the mistaken idea that if she separated the two young creatures, the power of the remaining one would be weakened. To an extent this turned out to be true, but not quite the way in which Miss Carnegie foresaw in her imagination. Rachel had been left with the other children on one such occasion when they were in the playground quite legitimately and Alice had been gently urged to go and have a talk with Miss Carnegie and Miss Felicity. Miss Eileen had been left to supervise the children from the warmth and security of the classroom whilst the children played tag outside in the cold bright air of a November morning. Now, a factor in Miss Carnegie's reasoning had been overlooked and that was the unusual behaviour of one of the little boys in the school. This was a certain Kevin, who was now almost a year older than the two girls as well as the eldest pupil in the school. Until our two girls had been enrolled at the beginning of that term, he had been top dog, alpha male, numero uno, Mr.Big, the man, etc. and with two of his younger allies had ruled the roost of this little nursery school. Not that he had ever done anything as adventurous as was the case this term, but still he had had the respect and acceptance of the other members of this pastoral community and he had managed to harbour a lingering resentment in his small breast until that morning when two events coincided with the unfortunate ensuing result. The prime cause of this will become clear at a later stage, but the immediate result of his excited state was this window of opportunity to re-establish his power centre. Seizing the day, he rallied both his supporters and made a sudden frontal attack on Rachel, a thing he would never have dared to even contemplate had he been his usual self and had Alice been there as well. Rachel was completely taken by surprise although she responded well enough, but without any warning she had a comparatively large boy kneeling on her chest and pummelling away at her, while his two more timid and smaller acolytes landed a few cowardly kicks for good measure. Rachel had managed to get in a couple of telling punches but Kevin was a street scrapper and had been well taught by his two older brothers so she was getting quite some punishment herself. As this was the first time she had engaged with an opponent intent on doing real harm, she was at some disadvantage and would no doubt have come out of it fairly badly if Alice, having been released from an unsatisfactory conversation with Miss Carnegie and Miss Felicity, had not suddenly come out to the playground. Sizing up the situation with commendable promptitude, she had run straight over to the melee, pushed her way through the surge of infant spectators and clouting both the assistant attackers over the head, grabbed Kevin by the hair and yanked him off the recumbent body of her friend. She then proceeded to punish him quite scientifically while Rachel got up and revenged herself on the now screaming malefactor. The staff, Miss Eileen included, (having been startled into awareness that real life had other things to offer besides the antics of the characters in a bodice-ripper), came rushing out to rescue Kevin from the punishment which was being inflicted on him. They separated the combatants, told the two Kevin supporters to quieten down and Rachel and Alice to go inside with Miss Felicity who would ring up their mother, (it was Vera's turn then as Rachel's parents were away) and she would come and collect them. The two girls went meekly into the common room with Miss Felicity. where she first attended to their bruises with iodine and other suitable lotions and potions and then rang the garden centre and spoke to Vera.

Miss Carnegie looked after Kevin's wounds in the study and tried to get some sense out of him as to what had precipitated the disturbance. Kevin was almost inarticulate with rage, but the teacher gathered that the boy was mostly bitter about being worsted by a couple of stupid girls. Miss Carnegie was quite blunt with him and said that as he had obviously and with no provocation attacked Rachel when she was on her own which was a very cowardly thing to do and she had no sympathy with him. He said some rather rude words and Miss Carnegie slapped him very hard and said that if she ever heard him using words like that again to anybody, she would have him expelled, to which he replied that that was fine with him and she was a silly old cat and went to storm out of the room. Miss Carnegie grabbed hold of him and made him sit down while she tried to get in touch with his parents. (This sort of behaviour on the part of the teacher was an eminently suitable and understandable reaction to the unbridled hostility and rudeness shown to her, and at the time, the mid sixties, was accepted as such. Nowadays, some fifty or so years later, we are so civilised that the teacher would most probably be sued by the monstrous bully, lose her position and never be allowed to work with children again and might even be sent to prison, The newspapers would have a field day with screaming headlines about teacher brutality and all the rest of the nonsense but that's progress for you. Go figure!).

When Vera arrived Miss Eileen was reading to the now subdued children all seated correctly in their little chairs. She read to them from the Beatrix Potter books which had always been a favourite of hers. Dear Mama had introduced them to her and her sister all that time ago when people were kind and polite to each other and the world was a different place disturbed only by the horrendous Boche and his Hunnish ways. Vera marched straight into the common room and went over to the two girls who were sitting placidly side by side in an armchair several sizes too big for them. Rachel had an alarming black eye but other than that they seemed unharmed. "Hullo, Mummy," they chorused happily.

"Hullo, brats," she replied. kneeling down in front of them. "So what have you been up to?" she enquired. "Kevin hit me, so Alice hit him," Rachel explained succinctly. "Kevin bad boy," confirmed Alice. Vera turned to Miss Felicity.

"You called me back for this?" she said coldly.

"Have you seen what they did to Kevin?" Miss Felicity said almost tearfully. "I don't know how I'm going to explain that to his parents.

"Where is Kevin now," Vera demanded. "Have they taken him away on a stretcher, or a hearse, maybe?" Miss Felicity bridled.

"This is no laughing matter, you know. Children in my care have never come to any harm before your two girls came to my school. The other children just do what they tell them to do and we have lost all control over them. I can't go on like this. They are a very disruptive influence on the school. Also Kevin's parents are very important people in the village and I cannot afford to alienate them. They will put it about that I am not fit to run this school and then I'll have to close down and it will all be the fault of these.....these....." Words seem to fail her at this point, at least the words which were hovering on the tip of her tongue but which she knew she could never utter to the implacable face of their mother.

"...dear little children, I think you were going to say." Vera suggested helpfully. Miss Felicity drew enough courage to look defiance at Vera, who could easily guess what was going through the poor woman's mind.

"Look, don't let's get this out of proportion," Vera said soothingly. "I know my kids have a natural talent for taking over any occasion and getting everybody to do what they think they would really like to be doing but which they aren't doing at the moment, like being outside when you think they should be inside and all that sort of thing, but all things being equal, what's the harm? Also, why did Kevin attack Rachel in the first place?"

"I think you must ask him that yourself," Miss Felicity said. "He's in the study with Miss Carnegie at the moment. Shall we go in and talk to them?"

"Very well," Vera said. "Stay here, kids, I'll be back in a moment," she said to her little dears, who smiled benignly and stuck their tongues out in unison at her.

"Very charming, I'm sure," she said in response and they sniggered naughtily.

The schoolmistress led the way into the study that was further down the corridor which stretched along one side of the old building. When they entered the study, Miss Carnegie was putting the phone down and looked as if she had been having a most unpleasant time with the speaker at the other end.

"That was your mother on the phone," she said forbiddingly to Kevin, who was sitting sulkily on an upright chair nursing his wounds. He had a couple of bruises on his face, his hands and knees were grazed where the girls had flattened him onto the playground, his scalp was still sore from the rough handling he had received when Alice first dragged him off her friend, and of course his *amour propre* was seriously out of sorts.

"I'm not surprised at your bad manners or your foul language, young man," she said, breaking every taboo in the teacher/pupil relationship book which looks askance at any negative comments on a parent's behaviour by either party. "She's one of the rudest people I have ever come across and with those two wretched brothers of yours no wonder you're the way you are. Is your father like that, too?"

" 'E's gorn," muttered the unfortunate child.

"I'm not surprised. I would be gorn too if I had to put up with you lot," said the young lady tartly, also contradicting every unwritten convention in the annals of teacher behaviour towards their charges.

"Any road, she's coming up to fetch you home and good riddance, I say." She turned to her employer. "I expect you'll have a rough time with Mrs.Black when she turns up to collect Kevin," she said. "So I'll stay and keep you company until they've gone and then you can sack me if you want to."

"Oh, please, Miss Carnegie, Emma, I'm so sorry all this has happened. I don't know why Kevin is behaving like this. He's usually such a good little boy. What do you think has happened, Mrs.Darwin? We've never ever had anything like this. Oh dear. I expect Mrs.Black will be ever so cross. She's got to come such a long way and she won't want to have to come back later to fetch Kevin at the end of the day and oh dear what *shall* I do?" she appealed to Vera, who suggested she put the kettle on and made some tea and she would have a quiet word with the little boy and see if she could put him in a more agreeable mood. She went to sit beside the miserable child and murmured a few words to him. The other two ladies noticed the child relaxing enough to take the thumb out of his mouth and turn to look at the strange lady who was talking so quietly to him. They also saw her sit up a bit straighter and after a few more consolatory words and a kindly rub on his back she got up and came over to speak to them out of the range of his hearing.

"Will his mother bring a doctor with her?" she asked. "Because of one thing I am sure and that is that he reacted this way because he has taken some form of drug. I don't know what it is, but his pupils are dilated and his behaviour would account for an amphetamine or something of that nature. I am sure he needs medical attention."

"But he's hardly four years old," protested Emma Carnegie, "Where on earth would he have got such a thing from?"

"Has he got older brothers?" asked Vera.

"Of course," said Miss Felicity. "Brian's eight and I think Joe is sixteen or thereabouts."

The ladies looked at each other, then at the little boy who had fallen into a doze in his chair.

"I think you must send for an ambulance immediately. Tell them it's a suspected overdose and the child must have found it somewhere. If I'm wrong, well, I'll give a contribution to the ambulance people, but if I'm right in my guess then we may have saved his life. Here, let me telephone."

Vera had rightly surmised that Miss Felicity was completely thrown by the situation and although Emma Carnegie still had her senses about her, she was not reacting quickly enough for Vera's satisfaction. She dialled 999 and spoke authoritatively into the instrument.

The ambulance preceded Mrs.Black by some five minutes by which time Kevin had been carted off to the A & E department of the cottage hospital. The ambulance men agreed that it looked very like a drug induced coma and reckoned they had got there just in time.

"Well, that would account for his unusual behaviour, of course," Emma Carnegie said. "I'm so sorry I did not understand that immediately. What kind of teacher am I not to be able to spot that type of behaviour?"

"There's no point in beating yourself up, you know," Vera said kindly. "One doesn't come across four-year-olds on drugs every day of the week. I expect this is the first time and somehow he's got hold of something of one of his brother's or even eaten some exotic plant from the garden or the woods which has caused the onset of this episode. Is that Mrs.Black now?" she asked as they heard a car drive up to the school gates.

"Oh yes, what on earth are we going to say to her?" Miss Felicity's colour faded from her face and Vera thought she was going to faint, but she managed to get the overwrought woman into a chair before she collapsed onto the floor.

"We, or rather I, am going to tell her that her son has been taken into hospital and that I am going to drive her there and she is going to tell the doctor everything she knows concerning any possible drugs being brought into the house or, failing that, what access Kevin might have had to poisonous substances. This will speed up the process of determining what caused the episode and what they need to do for the child. You look after my children and I'll go and talk with Mrs. Black."

Alice and Rachel had got tired of waiting for anybody to come and play with them, so they opened the door of the common room and went into the class-room where Miss Eileen was still reading Miss Potter's stories about her countryside menagerie to the rest of the school. Most of the children had fallen asleep because Miss Eileen had a singularly monotonous voice which often eventuated in causing Miss Eileen herself to nod off, so our two little girls entered the classroom unobserved, sat down on the floor, and being fairly exhausted themselves after their morning's exertions, fell asleep in each other's arms.

Vera, having delivered Kevin's mother to the tender mercies of an intensely irritated intern, returned post haste to the nursery school. Alice and Rachel were not in the place where Vera had last seen them, so she stormed into the study to find Miss Carnegie and Miss Felicity sharing a pot of tea and commiserating with each about the morning's hullaballoo. Where? she demanded, were her children. Emma Carnegie enlightened her.

"I think I had better take them home now, don't you?"

"They're all right for the moment, as you can see," Emma assured her. "And they're fast asleep," she added, "for a change!"

Vera agreed to go back to work after being assured that her girls were completely absolved from any repercussions and the two teachers thanked her for her prompt and resourceful action getting Kevin into safe hands. The doctor had taken all the necessary steps to minimise the effects of the drug on the little boy and a policeman was going to go back with the mother to find out how Kevin had got hold of the substance in the first place. He'd managed to have a gentle word with Kevin in a lucid moment before he dropped off to sleep again. Apparently the boy had found a screw of kitchen foil which when opened had revealed some white powder. He had taken an incautious sniff of the contents and some of the powder had got up his nose and made him sneeze. "Probably saved his life, that sneeze," the constable had averred. "Any higher dose and he could have been a goner. Just as well that Mrs.Darwin spotted his condition!"

"Just as well, indeed," agreed the doctor.

"So all's well that ends well," commented Tom that evening on being regaled with the history of the day's events. They were having a latish supper after having fed and bathed the children, anointed some of the bruises with either iodine or arnica lotion and also dosed them with homœopathic arnica pills, read them a bedtime story and generally made a fuss of them. They were tired little people after such a strenuous day and dropped off to sleep very quickly.

"Yes. I rang Mrs.Black. She's a nice woman really, but the husband was a heavy drinker and a boor to boot, so he left when Kevin arrived, said he couldn't put up with all that baby stuff again and went off with some popsy he'd met in Bristol. Good riddance, she told me. Apart from Joe, who was going through the usual bad boy behaviour that seemed *de rigeur* amongst the youth of the day, she said they were doing all right and although Kevin got some bullying from his elder brothers, they were quite a happy family. She was very shaken about the drug situation of course. Joe had admitted having a small amount of cocaine which he had experimented with. The policeman got the name of his supplier in return for not arresting him, and warned him about the danger he was putting himself and his family into by even associating with people who peddled drugs. He added that it was more than likely that the substance Joe had bought had been cut with some poisonous pesticide or other that could make him very ill or even kill him. He also pointed out to Joe that having such stuff at his home where inquisitive younger brothers could get hold of it was tantamount to giving them a loaded revolver to play with. By this time Joe was so terrified and wretched with remorse that the policeman thought it unlikely that he would ever go near the stuff again. He told him that he and his colleagues would be keeping an eye on him and if he felt like spreading the word amongst his friends about the bad effects of drugs, it would go a long way to rehabilitating him in the eyes of the police

CHAPTER IV

Rebecca and Joseph returned in time for Christmas and the children went down with the chicken pox which was doing the rounds of the village and had occasioned the closure of the nursery and local primary school until the end of that Christmas term. Both young girls seemed able and content to sleep through the worst of it and only needed a few applications of calamine lotion before the blisters had healed over.

Both parents were motivated by this event to think that their progeny might be better off not attending primary school and being home educated. The two ladies had had previous experience as teachers and were equipped with all the necessary qualifications. What was also important was that between Vera and Toms's expert knowledge of botany and biochemistry and Rebecca and Joseph's medical training was a fund of practical language and literary skills for the girls to draw on. Anything else could easily be accessed via the public library or the numerous encyclopaedias dotted about the two houses. It was an idea to be seriously considered. Alice and Rachel, while they enjoyed every moment of being outside playing in the gardens and the neighbouring woodlands, were also gluttons for knowledge. They took to reading as ducks to water and by the time they left the nursery school they were literary fluent. Once they got immersed in a book, it would be difficult to drag them away from it. Peter Rabbit and Benjamin Bunny soon gave way to Doctor Dolittle which was succeeded by Just William, Swallows and Amazons, E.Nesbit and all the old favourites of childhood. These were soon superseded by Sexton Blake, Bulldog Drummond, Edgar Wallace, the Saint, Arséne Lupin and of course Sherlock Holmes. Tom had kept almost all his own childhood library and any new additions were almost automatically added as they came to be published. This, incidentally, was for Tom's entertainment as well! By the time they were eight years old they had read almost everything by Dickens, Wilkie Collins, Samuel Richardson, Butler, Sterne and Fielding. Then they discovered Robert Surtees, (demanding the illustrated editions) and from there made a quantum leap to Marcel Proust by way of Marcel Aymé, Balzac and Gustave Flaubert. Their pursuit of literary novelties and experiences did nothing to hamper their more mundane activities or of honing their fighting skills. They developed their own strategies of jungle warfare in and around the stretches of woodland and ancient forest which lay between their two homes and they practised accuracy and co-ordination of hand and eye in the casting of stones and other objects at specific targets. They never tried to hit a bird or an animal, but they never minded attacking each other and learning boxing techniques which they followed on videos and martial art routines which they culled from books from the library and of course the classic kung fu films of Bruce Lee and other masters of the genre. They could have done with a teacher, of course, but both the Darwins were highly trained agents and gave them lessons and advice when they were home and not caught up with their market garden business. Joseph and Rebecca had their fair share of fighting skills but did not want to get involved with that side of the girls' education, being content to teach them healing techniques and instructions on how to deal with emergency situations when there was no professional help to hand.

The end result was that the two young people had an excellently rounded education which furnished them with a broader set of skills than are usually achieved by a more formal system. However, they all agreed that when they reached secondary school age they would enrol at the local grammar school which was just about to become an independent and well within walking distance from their homes. It had a good reputation and the standard of teaching appeared more than acceptable to parents and daughters. It would provide the girls with a wider social sphere and a better knowledge of the world they lived in.

At the beginning of the summer of the year when they were to enter the school, a change happened in their relationship. It was quite simple. Until that tine they had rough and tumbled about like two happy tomboys with no inhibitions about each other than that they were the best of friends and never more happy than when they were together, either reading or playing, fighting, climbing trees, having picnics or horse riding. For their tenth birthday Tom had bought them a share in a couple of ponies that were stabled with a local stud farm and riding school. They adored the animals and learned from the professionals how to look after them and keep them healthy and how to muck out their quarters and make sure that the saddles were comfortable and that they were not injured by badly adjusted tackle.

One day in June of that year, prior to their enrolment at the newly converted independent school, they were making their way back from the stables by their usual eccentric route, tracking each other through the undergrowth and ambushing each other at frequent intervals. Either Alice ambushed Rachel or Rachel leapt upon Alice but they rolled down a bank of ferns and tussled about in a grassy clearing at the bottom of the incline. They had got each other in a stranglehold with Rachel on top of Alice when an totally unexpected change came over each of them virtually instantaneously. One minute they were two tomboys having their usual scrap and then, as they looked into each other's eyes, they both became aware that the person they were looking at was at the same time a total stranger and someone they had known all of their lives. Their hands, which had been round each other's throats slowly relaxed and Rachel allowed herself to relax so that she was lying along the whole length of Alice's body and that it was a most pleasing sensation.

Alice had also relaxed her hands which had been around Rachel's throat and they curled gently round the back of her friend's head and brought it down to lie against her cheek. For the first time they were aware of the hearts beating in their bodies and the blood flowing through each others veins and arteries and the life force warming each other and mingling in the auras which had melded together forming a vibrant energy embracing them both like a cocoon. They lost all notion of the passage of time and luxuriated in this unsolicited but most welcome novel experience. When the moment came Rachel rolled off Alice and they both stood up, joined hands, kissed each other gently on the lips and walked slowly and happily back to Alice's house.

It probably hadn't been all that long since time had seemed to stand still, because it was about 5.00 when they entered the kitchen door. Vera was at the sink, doing housewifely things.

"Help yourself to some tea," she said, glancing at them as she busied herself with some washing up. "It'll probably need some hot water."

"Thanks, Mum, we had a mug at the stables," Alice said dreamily. The two girls smiled at her and made their way upstairs. "Supper will be late tonight," Vera called after them. A faint OK was heard as the two went into the bedroom, undressed and got into bed together. There was nothing unusual in this as they always slept in the same bed and had done so since they were babies. Today, of course, was somewhat different. They lay gazing into each other's eyes until they gently fell asleep. When they woke a couple of hours later, Rachel was nestling in Alice's arms and they were both feeling the sort of benign ecstasy which always seems so indestructible at the time. At a given moment some time later they both got out of the bed and dressed themselves. They then went down to supper. Neither of them said anything nor did their parents, except for commonplace remarks about commonplace things. The two girls retired after supper, saying that they were both very exhausted and needed some extra sleep.

"I wonder what's exhausted those two," said Jerry. "They were extraordinarily quiet this evening. Have they fallen in love or something? They both had sort of daft soppy looks on their faces all evening. Odd, I call it."

"The problem you have, dear brother," said Tom, "is that you have a very limited imagination, not to say a very naive understanding of the human psyche. The expressions you are so ignorantly referring to as 'daft and soppy' are the expressions of two young people who are becoming aware of the wonder and complexity of all things, of which you, brother mine, are an exceedingly primitive example."

"Heavens," Jerry exclaimed. "*rem acu tetigisti, frater meum.* You have characterised me to a nicety. I am, as ever, eternally in your debt!"

"One thing he's right about," observed Vera, "and that is that those two have suddenly fallen for each other as totally as is possible for nigh on eleven-year-olds, that is"

"I think you are right, Vera. Perhaps it's just as well they are both the same sex, as I am reluctant to become a grandparent at my age, even if I'll never see forty again."

"Not really the point, Becky," replied Vera. "I'm sure they would be sensible and knowledgeable enough not to confuse the issue while they have so much to live for at the moment. But I think they'll do very well in any case."

"They've always loved each other,," said Joseph. "We've known that from the beginning. Do you remember we talked about that, Tom, when they were only a few months old?"

"Yes, we thought that they were a bit like Damon and Pythias, or rather, I thought that. I can't recall what you thought, Joe."

"Oh, I just followed your guidance as always," Joseph murmured philosophically.

"God help us, this is turning into a gay lovefest," Vera said to Rebecca. "Come out to the kitchen with me, Becky and we can make passionate love while doing the dishes!"

"Charmed, I'm sure," Rebecca responded. "Shall I go and fetch my dildo?"

"Ladies! Ladies! and Ladies!" protested Jerry. "Remember we are all died-in-the-wool heterosexually oriented people and let us have no more of this tasteless frivolity."

"Please yourself," said Vera, getting up. "I'm going to put the coffee on. Coming, Rebecca?"

"I'll give you a hand or two," said Rebecca following her friend into the kitchen with a stack of dirty plates. "You wash, me dry?"

"Fine by me," Vera was already filling the sink with hot water. "Thank God for this lovely Aga," she said. "It was worth every penny having it converted."

"You're not worried about the girls, are you?" Rebecca asked her.

"Hell, no. Basically it's none of our business and I don't think anybody should make any comment or give any sign that we find anything the slightest unusual about their behaviour. I'm sure they won't go moping around being a laughing stock to the whole village. They've got far too much pride for that."

"I'm sure they have," Rebecca agreed, "but you know how strong emotions can be at any age, let alone at a time when they are not fully developed and have learnt how to control their behaviour in public."

"Becky!" Vera apostrophised her friend. "Have you never noticed how those two never give anything away, however disturbed or even enraged they may be feeling. Or even, come to think of it, embarrassed, either. You weren't there when I accidentally knocked over a whole display of china in our local emporium, were you? The question is rhetorical," she continued without a pause. "I clumsily upset a whole dinner service, smashing many of its most decorative pieces to smithereens. The manager came raging out and in less time than it takes to tell I had twisted the whole scene round so that it was all the store's fault that the display was there in the first place, it was a potential death-trap, a public hazard and my lawyer would be in touch with them for the shock and inconvenience we had been put through and my daughter might have been cut or even blinded by shards of pottery flying about and I was taking her to A&E as she was in shock as he could very well see and look at her white face and come along you poor thing it's better to walk than wait for the ambulance and I was out of there before he could get another word in. Forget that it was totally outrageous of me and I should be ashamed of myself and I was, because I did send them anonymously an enormous amount of cash with a typed explanation which I think probably covered it quite well. The reason I'm telling you this is that not once did Alice so much as turn a hair or give any sign of embarrassment. She didn't even blush while I spouted all this crap at the poor man, but afterwards when we were well away from the scene she told me exactly what she thought of my actions that morning. She also went a fiery red and she actually hissed at me, and she was only five years old at the time. I was almost terrified, but more I was so intrigued that all this was just being kept in check until the right moment came when I wasn't driving the car, we were not within earshot of anybody else and we were also of course well away from the shop. Such venom and rage, you've no idea. So, I think she is a natural at concealing her emotions and temperamentally as cool as ice when she wants to be. I think your Rachel is the same. They will only reveal their feeling for each other to each other. Neither of them tittle-tattle or gossip about other people, nor do I think they feel bad things about them. You remember that business we had with poor little Kevin Black who'd cleverly managed to snort a whiff of cocaine up his hooter and went into a homicidal attack on Rachel? They completely forgave him even before we explained to them why the attack had happened. They are so cute, those two, that I would trust them with my life."

"My, what an accolade. Perhaps you should commit that to print and hang it over their bed"

Vera flicked some water at her while stacking up some more dishes for drying.

"So what happened after this tirade? Were you down on your knees pleading forgiveness or did you just belt her one?"

"Neither, you idiot!" Vera laughed outright. "I just apologised, explained that I didn't want to be caught up in some possible publicity stunt or newspaper report, gave her a cuddle and promised to compensate the store for the damage I had caused.

She was satisfied with that and had the good sense not to cross question me about my motives as I don't think any of us were ready at that time to discuss our careers with them, do you?" She looked at her friend meaningfully. "I think that we will have to talk about it some time soon, though."

"I reckon," Rebecca said placidly, "that they have a pretty good idea already of the work we have to do and our responsibilities."

"Yes well, we might discuss this with the chaps later. Let's leave those plates to dry off a bit. Go and talk to the boys while I bring the coffee in," she said while preparing a tray with cups, milk and sugar to accompany the percolator.

"You're a very good actress, aren't you," Rebecca said appreciatively. "You brought that whole scene in the store to life, but I would never have thought to see Alice as you describe her there. She's always so smiley and happy looking. Do you think Rachel gets like that, too?"

"Those two have hidden depths, I'm telling you,"Vera said darkly. "And I am a good actress. You have to be to survive in sone of the places we go, which means that you are also a very good actress, my nice, kind, gentle friend. I think we each have a dark side to us; we've seen too much not to have one. It doesn't hurt to acknowledge it either."

"Meaning?" Rebecca raised her eyebrows with a wry smile on her face.

"Ach, nothing much. I'm just rambling. Let's take this in for the menfolk or they'll be getting all crotchety. Men! Huh!"

"Women! Wow!" Jerry had heard Vera's last remarks as the ladies came back to the dining-room bearing coffee, cake, cups and plates between them.

"And why not?" was Tom's answer.

CHAPTER V

The elders finally agreed to give their daughters a general outline of the clandestine side of their frequent trips abroad, mainly to advise them of the inherent dangers of ever discussing their parents' foreign assignments with anybody else, apart from acknowledging the obvious if the matter ever came up in conversation. It would also help them to formulate the type of response they could give when and if their teachers wanted them to write essays on their domestic situations. The education system often used this as an excuse for copping out of suitable subject matter for young adolescents to talk about in class.

"Yes, you don't want them blurting out to the whole school that Mummy and Daddy are really secret agents with licenses to kill and deep cover training as government assassins, do you? I mean it would shoot their social status through the roof but the repercussions would be horrid," said Jerry.

Tom gave his brother a cold look.

"Even though it is only a thousand to one chance that somebody has a distance mike pointing at us, I beg you to remember that it is never a good idea to make any open mention of our work at any time and not even talk in your sleep or think about it, is that clear, Jerry?"

"Okay, I'm sorry, I thought we were safe here. I mean, do you seriously think that there's somebody up a tree listening to us?" They were strolling through an open sward of lush green grass bordered by the surrounding woodland, the nearest tree being at least a hundred yards away.

"We always think there is somebody out there spying on us which is why we've stayed alive so long. Don't start getting careless, Jerry, or I will have you taken off for a refresher course and you would not enjoy that."

"Yes, I do forget, sometimes. It all seems such a phantasy, of which I'm not a part, that I forget it's deadly serious."

"Jerry," said Joseph calmly. "You are as much a part of this as we are. If we are harmed, so will you be. So will our children and we must protect them as best as we can and you, Jerry, must also protect yourself. In any case, you are, I'm sorry to say, our weakest link. We have been trained to withstand much pressure. You haven't and the sort of people who inhabit that part of our world are merciless."

"So your part is an exercise in complete forgetfulness," Vera said firmly. "Never think about it and never bring the subject up. We are market gardeners, plain and simple and travel sometimes to find new species. Rebecca and Joseph are respected medical researchers and fully qualified doctors who lend a hand when necessary to overseas health agencies and NGOs. I'm sorry if that doesn't satisfy your restless nature but if you want to join the Service then you should apply in the usual manner or become a traffic warden or something."

This was an unkind thrust and Jerry flinched, but he realised they talked good sense and he was not going to put his brother and his two families into jeopardy on account of any loose talk. Just then the two girls ran up with a wounded blackbird they had just found. Rebecca examined it as best she could and thought that it was probably just stunned.

"Where did you find it" she asked them. They told her that it was just lying on the edge if the green. They had noticed it as it fell from somewhere inside the tree coverage.

****

The week prior to their first day at school was mostly occupied with kitting them out with their school uniforms and acceptable footwear. The problem with finding the right sized shoes for them was compounded because for past years they had either worn no shoes or open-toed sandals so that their feet were unusually wide and strongly individual. The solution was to fit them with boy's shoes which they were not entirely comfortable with because they felt the restrictions that normally are felt by anybody used to having bare feet. They had ceased to resemble each other the older they grew and by now were totally individual. Alice was slender, wiry, blond-haired, blue-eyed and fair-skinned with a small and beautiful facial structure. She would normally wear her hair in pig-tails on either side of her head except when engaged in some strenuous activity when she would roll it into a tight bun at the back. Her friend had developed into a rather sturdy looking girl with a darker skin and raven hair which she wore bunched behind her head.

Their arrival at the school gate on the first day of the new term created quite a stir of interest. They looked very fresh and attractive in their school uniforms, (red blazers, white shirts and school ties, dark skirts and black shoes). They were greeted with a mixture of friendly interest and veiled hostility. Their reputations as the two wild girls who lived in the woods and had been raised by wolves preceded them of course. At lunchtime that first day, they came out to the playground to be surrounded by a gathering of their peers and confronted by a large bulky youth some two years older and at least ten inches taller than either of them. They looked at him impassively. "What you might call the acne of perfection," Alice murmured.

"Ha, ha, bloody funny," responded the afflicted youth glaring balefully at them. "Are you two lezzies, then?" he demanded. Rachel turned to Alice,

"What's a lezzie?" she asked innocently of her friend.

"I'm not sure, but I think the word is a vulgarisation of the word Lesbian," Alice responded. Ignoring the catcalls, she added clearly, "I imagine that he wants to know whether we come from the island of Lesbos. Is that what you want to know?" she enquired of the spotty youth.

"Wotcha talking about?" he shouted at her.

"More to the point, what exactly are you talking about?"

"Are you two, you know, do you do it together?" Alice looked at him coldly.

"Do you think you could rephrase that into proper English?" she said. "If I am right in understanding what you are saying, you are being very impertinent and it is none of your concern."

"Oooh, very impertinent am I?" he mocked, and everybody screamed with laughter. "You were seen kissing each other in the woods last week, so there,"

"Kissy kissy, who's a sissy," chanted the crowd.

"Don't you kiss your friends?" Alice asked him innocently. "Don't any of you ever kiss your friends?" she addressed the crowd. "Don't your parents ever kiss you? You must all be very lonely people if you cannot demonstrate affection for each other." But the crowd of adolescents went on jeering as the two girls made to move away from their tormentors. The spotty youth stood in their way.

"We don't like pervs in our school, see!" he faced them truculently. "So you'd better get yourselves a couple of boyfriends before the week's out or it's going to be the worst for you, see?"

Alice looked him straight in the eye.

"Are you putting yourself forward as a candidate for such an honour?" she enquired gently. He preened himself.

"You could do worse," he said smugly.

"It would be possible," Rachel said thoughtfully, "if a syphilitic Mongolian pederast were to present himself, but barring that, I'm afraid, you really won't do, you know." He was unsure exactly how to respond to this remark offered, as it was, in such gently rejecting tones.

"The trouble is, you see," Alice took up the complaint. "You are possibly one of the most unpleasant, foul smelling and disgusting individuals we have so far met today and if you are an example of suitable escorts on these premises, then we would have to reject your advances. As it is we have no wish to establish any such relations so your demands will not be met and would you kindly stand out of our way as this conversation is now terminated."

It would have been more seemly for the youth to have acceded to this polite request but, sadly for him, he couldn't resist. Encouraged by the crowd of children he moved towards them. They took a cautious step back and found themselves with their backs literally against the wall of the building. A look of gloating satisfaction came over his face.

" 'Ow would you like to find your pretty new uniforms all messed up with rolling on the ground and your pretty little curls cut orf yer pretty little heads?" he demanded belligerently.

"I take it that the question is rhetorical?" Rachel said calmly. "He really is rather tall for us, don't you think," she informed Alice. Both girls were keeping a steady gaze on the pugnacious youth while his supporters jeered and called for blood.

"I do agree," Alice replied. "Definitely needs some reduction. Too many calories, I reckon."

"Accounts for the pimples," Rachel diagnosed, bringing the toe of her right foot sharply into contact with the diaphragm of her interlocutor who, doubling up with the sudden acute agony inflicted on that area of his body, had the wind knocked out of him. His face descended rapidly in the direction of Alice's open fisted strike which sent him reeling backwards into the crowd, blood pouring from his broken nose. Rachel knelt beside the fallen boy and, fishing out a rather grubby handkerchief from his pocket, placed it on his nose. She then guided his hand to hold it firmly in place and helped him to his feet. The mixed crowd of male and female pupils were shocked into silence by the suddenness and ferocity of this activity, all of which had taken no more than a couple of seconds. They fell back as the two girls helped the sobbing boy from the playground. The headmistress and most of the staff had been observing this confrontation from the safety of their common room. As the two girls disappeared escorting the stricken blood-stained youth between them, the headmistress and her senior master moved briskly out of the common room and towards the changing rooms where they correctly surmised the trio would be found.

Rachel was seated on a bench next to the boy and holding a length of roller towel soaked in cold water to his face. The flow of blood had virtually been staunched but he was still somewhat in shock and very white about the parts visible behind the toweling. Rachel was talking gently to him and his breathing seemed to be fairly calm. Alice had taken her shirt off and was rinsing it in cold water as the teachers strode in. "What on earth do you think you are doing, young lady?" demanded the senior master furiously.

"Dress yourself decently this instant. And what do you think you are doing, Katz? This boy should be seen by a doctor immediately. This is no time to be playing at being at hospital nurse." He made to move Rachel away from her patient. Rachel turned a cold eye on him.

"I have reset his broken nose, and if you interfere with what I am doing here, this boy will have a crooked nose for the rest of his life unless he has surgery. Is that what you want?"

"How dare you, you impudent child," he stormed at her. "Move away at once. And you, Darwin, put that shirt back on at once."

"Mr Roberts," Alice said politely. "Katz's parents are fully qualified doctors, you know, and Rachel has a nursing certificate which she acquired after a rigorous examination by the BMA. I think that you must acknowledge that she has treated her patient with commendable promptitude and skill. If she had not been present, this unfortunate boy would have lost a lot of blood and probably been permanently scarred. When I have finally washed the blood off my shirt I will of course resume wearing it, damp though it is. I will then have to rinse out Rachel's shirt, so I would be grateful if you would retire when she has released her patient to your care, as she will have to divest herself of the article and it would be most improper if you were present when she does so - that is, unless you have a medical degree, of course."

Roberts was rendered almost, but not quite, speechless. He went very red and both girls looked at him with some alarm as he started spluttering. The Headmistress saved the situation by telling him firmly that he should follow this advice if Katz was ready to hand over her patient to him. Rachel gently stood the boy up and still holding the toweling over his face handed him over to the enraged teacher.

"You will have to be very careful to keep this in place," she said. "If you apply about half a cup of cold water to the outside of the toweling in the nasal area in abut ten minutes and carefully let him peel it away from his nose he should be all right. He might also need a plaster to keep the nose in position until it heals so he should see a doctor very soon," she suggested. Mr. Roberts gulped and choked back whatever bile was rising on his gorge. Fortunately the Headmistress took charge of the boy and led them both away from the changing-rooms. Roberts couldn't stop fulminating.

"Those two brats are insufferable. I will not have my authority flouted like this. Being told off by a couple of first year pupils and on their first day at this school! They break this poor boy's nose and then play hospital nurses. Really, Headmistress, I think you will have to get those two out of here."

"I don't think I want to do that quite yet, Mr. Roberts," said the Headmistress firmly. "Moreover," she added, having settled the now very quiet boy into a chair in her study and drawing the other teacher out of earshot. "This 'poor boy' is the fourth form school bully and richly deserved what he got this morning and well you know it. Perhaps we might see some improvement in young Fletcher Arkwright's academic performance now that he's been brought down a peg or two. You leave those two young ladies alone. I know their parents and they are tough people. Also, I might add, in spite of that piece of impudent flimflam about young Katz's so-called nursing certificates, her parents are highly respected medical professionals, used to treating war wounds and other severe traumas and have no doubt passed on a considerable amount of knowledge to their daughter and her friend. I cannot fault them for their behaviour and I also thought that they dealt with your indignation with great astuteness and even grace. I think they are going to make a difference to this school and it's been a long time coming."

"What *do* you mean?" he replied angrily. "What has been a long time coming?"

"Bullying," she replied bluntly. "Arkwright isn't the only malefactor. I have only been the headmistress of this school for a day, but I am very disturbed by the atmosphere of bullying, cliquey gangs and favouritism which has become endemic. Teaching standards may be high but that is no compensation for the unfair treatment meted out to many of the less advantaged children. This is not Eton or Harrow or any of those institutions where barbarity is held up as an ideal for the making of tomorrow's leading citizens and captains of industry. Those places teach the favourites how to bully so that they can practice on their weaker brethren. Our school must be a place of equal opportunity for all. We've got enough leaders of the British Empire who haven't got anyone to harass without creating more of them here. I dare say you are of the opinion, with many others of your generation, that fostering a climate of the survival of the fittest will equip our young people with the necessary tools for success, but I am sure you will agree that a nation of slaves ruled by autocratic entrepreneurs is not fit for a civilised society. People will not tolerate it any longer. We have had two major wars where millions of young and able people of both sexes have been slaughtered and all on account of the very attitudes you have displayed this morning."

Jeremiah Roberts, Assistant Head Teacher, was shocked and outraged at his colleague's remarks. She held up a hand. "Please let us not get into this any further until this boy has been taken care of." She went over to the now silent and glum-looking child.

"Come along, Fletcher. I'll take you down to Nurse for a check-up and if you are still feeling unwell, I will ring for a taxi to take you home. Will your mother or anybody else be in your house at the moment? I'll ring them shall I?" She continued without waiting for an answer. The boy's downcast expression was evidence enough that he had no wish to return to his class that day. At that moment the bell went for the start of the afternoon classes and the children could be heard going to their allotted places. Roberts disappeared in the direction of his classroom and the headmistress led the boy down to the first aid room so that Nurse could have a look at him and make an evaluation of his condition.

"Bit of shock. No lasting damage. Hot drink with plenty of sugar. Send him home."

Nurse was a fifty something virago from Yorkshire, who disliked children, especially boys and more particularly bullies of either sex. The unfortunate pupil was dispatched homewards in a taxi after his nose had been plastered over and told not to return until he had seen his family's doctor and been given a clean bill of health. On his return he was to present himself to the Headmistress half an hour before school started and before he had spoken to anybody else on pain of expulsion if he did not keep strictly to this instruction. A note was given him to present to his parents and a warning that his parents would be telephoned later that day and the contents of the note discussed with them and did he understand that? He nodded glumly.

"Very well, then," the Head said quite kindly to him. "Don't be too alarmed. Just go along with what I have asked you to do and everything will be all right for you. Do you understand?" Glum nod. "You are going to have to change your attitude," she continued. "It won't work any more this way you see, and you will find that in future you will be much happier with friends rather than with fear as your weapon of choice." He looked a bit nonplussed at that, but muttered a 'yes Miss' as he got into the taxi.

Alice and Rachel had tidied themselves up and rid themselves of the telltale bloodstains as best they could and hoped the shirts would dry off as soon as possible.

"An iron would have been welcome," Rachel murmured to her friend as they made their way into the classroom.

"So would a bit of time to have our sandwiches," Alice replied. "I am exceedingly hungry and my stomach is probably going to start rumbling soon."

"Well, at least we'll be giving them some entertainment," Rachel said philosophically. "One wonders what treats are in store for us later."

"One wonders indeed!"

As it happened neither of the girls' stomachs betrayed much discomfort and indeed the afternoon's lessons passed pleasantly enough. Both girls had the good sense not to reveal anything out of the ordinary in the general way of knowledge of the various subjects on the curriculum. They were well enough equipped to have been placed in classes for pupils at least two years ahead of their allotted places, but they sensibly thought it wise to keep a low profile and not force any issues unless they became intolerable. It never hurts to revise subjects as long as the revision doesn't interfere with the advance of knowledge.

CHAPTER VI

The story of Fletcher Arkwright's comeuppance naturally spread like wildfire and although the two friends gained much kudos and became popular in a quiet sort of way, there were some who resented this popularity and hankered for their downfall. Consequently, and because of their finely tuned antennae, they were circumspect in their movements, especially after school and on their homeward journeys. It was about three weeks into the term that they noticed a suspicious huddle of some of the older boys who kept glancing towards them during the break as they sat eating their lunch at one of the benches dotted around the playground.

"I think they're gearing themselves up for a bit of a fight after school, don't you reckon?" Rachel remarked.

"Yep, that Causten fellow seems to have some animus against us," Alice said. "He kept trying to trip me up at gym yesterday. If I hadn't been prepared, he might have caused me a serious mischief. I think we're going to have to deal with him with a considerable amount of prejudice."

"Hey ho," Rachel said philosophically. "Let's hope it happens well away from the school grounds, otherwise we'll have to answer some very awkward questions."

"Let's make for the woods lickety split, and then we'll be on our own territory. We'll stash our satchels in the oak-tree safe. If we go fast enough they won't see us do that and then we can collect them afterwards."

"Also our blazers. It's warm enough not to need them and we don't want them messed up. How many of them are there, do you think?"

"A good half dozen at least. Perhaps we should ask for some help. How about young Bobby Flint and his mate Teddy? They look as if they wouldn't mind getting their hands dirty."

"Tell you what, I think we should just keep this private. We can manage six of them and if they bring any more they'll probably run for it when they see what's happening to their mates. Also I don't think it's a good idea to get up a gang, otherwise we'll be in danger of relying on them in the future. We'll just have to settle this once and for all."

Alice conceded the point and they finished their lunches while keeping an eye on the conspirators who broke up their meeting but couldn't resist making threatening signs to the two girls. The leader of the pack, Will Causten, came over to them. "You're for it, you two pervs," he said bluntly. "You was told to behave yourselves and we don't want you in this school, see."

"I don't really think it's got anything to do with you and we're certainly not going to stay away just to please you, so you'd better just get used to it, hadn't you?" Alice said, standing up and putting her lunchbox in her satchel. "However, if you want to discuss it further, we can meet you in the woods in the clearing past the giant oak after school. Will that do for you? Or do you want us to put you into hospital now, so that the ambulance can pick up the pieces from the playground?"

"Don't be unkind, Alice," Rachel said. "Causten hasn't got his friends around him at the moment. It's all too one-sided, you must agree."

"Yes." Alice looked up placidly into the glowering face of the boy. "It's true what they say, though, isn't it? The bigger they are the harder they fall."

At that moment the bell went and the girls stood silently waiting for the boy to move away. He smirked at them. "You'll change your tune tonight, you'll see," he promised and turning abruptly away.

"Well, that's telling us," Rachel laughed. "Those guys - what are they like!"

When the final bell went for the end of classes for that day, the two girls kept well within the general exodus. Being in a different stream of children homeward bent, they managed to elude their predators until they were some way from the school gates. At a suitable juncture they made *post haste* to the woodland area where they had agreed to meet up with the gang.

"We could ambush them, couldn't we? Pick them off one by one maybe?" Rachel suggested.

"Let's just hide up a tree and wait. They'll probably all meet up here thinking that they're first and if they've got any trick up their sleeves like reinforcements we might learn something."

"To our advantage, no doubt. Yes, let's have a supply of ammo though. Just a few bits of dirt and gravel in our lunch boxes will do to throw in their faces for starters. We've got to get the edge somehow."

The girls quickly gathered whatever they could and filled the empty lunch boxes with a mixture of dust, leaf mould, twigs, small stones and earth which they then carried with them as they climbed up into the branches of the giant oak and waited for the arrival of their enemies. Some minutes passed.

"Have they chickened out?" Rachel whispered.

"Doubt it. They probably got delayed trying to find us after the bell went and think we're cowering in the loos trying to escape them. When they've searched that or got thrown out by the caretaker, they'll mosey on out here, so let's just be patient. I must say I would prefer to be on my way - "

"Shush!" Rachel cautioned. "I can hear them."

Causten and five of his teenage chums came into view quite openly and gathered round the bottom of the oak tree. "Bet you they've run off home," one of them said belligerently. "We'll have to get them tomorrow on their way to school. I know where they live so we can settle them then."

"No," Causten disagreed. "I bet you they'll come here. Those two wouldn't pass up on a fight. Thing is, they *will* do in future though."

"Dirty little lezzie shits," agreed the heavy built fourteen-year-old known as Jumbo to his friends. "Wouldn't mind giving that Jewish cunt a going over, mind!"

"P'raps we should do that instead of beating them up," one of the others suggested. "Give 'em a taste of a steaming hot cock for a change. That'd sort them."

"Yeah, bet they'd be gagging for it after that. Whatcher say, Dick?"

"No way," Causten said flatly. "If we did that, they'd report us to the fuzz or their parents and we'd be in dead shit."

"Our word against theirs!" Jumbo claimed.

"No," Carsten said again. "Stick to the plan. I don't want anything to do with those little tarts like that." He scowled at them. "You want to try that, do it in your own time. Today we mete out justice, right?"

"Right!" they agreed. Their leader looked at the watch on his wrist. "Where the fu -?" He stopped. "Listen! Someone's coming."

A black labrador bounded along the path closely followed by a middle-aged couple walking briskly in the same direction. "Afternoon!" they greeted the boys. "Lovely weather, what!" They murmured some vague response and Will Causten managed to bring out a sycophantic smile. The couple waved their walking sticks merrily at them and disappeared through the trees at the far end of the clearing. This minor diversion had enabled the two girls to position themselves strategically above the closely assembled gang and when all was quiet again, Alice shook an adjacent branch and called out to the assembled boys.

"Coo-ee!" she yodeled. The boys looked up open mouthed, the girls shook the contents of both their lunch boxes into their upturned faces and immediately followed this opening salvo by leaping on the two most threatening antagonists, Will Causten and the hefty Jumbo. To be dropped on by a solid well muscled body and in the space of a couple of seconds to be completely rendered *hors de combat* is a humbling experience for any commander and his lieutenant at the best of times; to have it so efficiently and scientifically achieved by two members of the weaker sex who are also several inches shorter and at least two years younger is totally humiliating. The two boys were totally humiliated. The girls also made short work of the remainder by a series of vicious punches and kicks to their temporarily blinded opponents. Through his pain, Will Causten became aware of Alice standing over him and reaching down to his left hand. She deftly removed the watch that adorned his wrist.

"You," she said sternly, "are a bully. This watch does not belong to you. It belongs to young Arthur Phillips, whom you have threatened and bullyragged ever since the beginning of this term. He is now under my protection." She stopped to look at Rachel who had been obliged to pacify one of the boys who looked as if he was about to stand up, by kicking him gently in the ribs. "Stay down, all of you," Rachel commanded. "You can get up when we have left but not before. The next person who moves will get kicked in the head and I won't answer for the consequences."

"Exactly," said Alice. "This goes for all of you, so listen up. If we have any more complaints from anybody about you bullying, stealing, demanding favours or sneaking on them, you will answer to us. Is that clear? Because we don't want to have to discuss this with any of you again."

"You might think of spreading that word around," Rachel added. "We will also report all bullying to the Headmistress as well as dealing with you privately, so make sure your chums know all about it. Any further attacks on us will land you in hospital or worse."

"What's more," Alice said grimly, "if any of you little boys ever so much as think of doing what this fat lump of excrement suggested to any female," she prodded the recumbent Jumbo with her toe, "we will pursue you to the ends of the earth and have you prosecuted in a court of law and you will be sent to prison for a very long time and your names will be mud."

"Of course, if you try it on us," Rachel said mildly, "we will cut off your testicles and shove them up your collective arses. Is *that* understood?"

The groans from the fallen had now subsided, although one boy was whimpering miserably. Rachel knelt down beside him. "When you get home, get some frozen veggie out of the fridge, wrap it in a tea towel and apply locally. You have got a fridge with frozen peas or something haven't you?"

The boy nodded miserably. "Fine. Well, if you're still worried, see your doctor. I wouldn't normally have kicked you there, but I didn't have many options at the time. You might think about changing your allegiance while you're at it." she added in a whisper. She stood up.

"I want my tea now," she said simply. "Bye zee bye, fellahs!" Alice gestured with her head towards the other side of the clearing where she could see the couple with the labrador standing watching them. She gave them a discreet wave and started walking towards them. Rachel collected their lunch boxes from where they had fallen, their blazers and satchels from the hole in the oak tree and trotted after her friend who was now following the couple who had retreated from the view of the gang who were picking themselves up and dispersing disconsolately homewards. The two girls caught up with the couple who had stopped for them once they were out of sight of the boys.

"That was pretty impressive," said the man, eying them in a friendly manner. The dog came snuffling up to them and the girls reached down to make friends.

"Practice makes perfect," Alice said sententiously.

"So I can tell," he retorted. "My name's Jack Hamilton. My wife, Betty." They shook hands with the couple.

"You own the Bedford Arms, don't you?" Alice asked politely. "My Dad has talked about you to us."

"Weren't you an RAF pilot during the war? First of the Few?" Rachel smiled at them.

"A bit early for me in fact," Jack said casually. "Wasn't quite old enough then. Joined up in '44 and flew bombers for my pains. What was all that scrap about? We heard what you said at the end but not what they said to you."

"Oh well, they thought we should be given a lesson in how to behave and how we should relate to each other and considered we were daughters of Satan or some such nonsense."

"Apparently we don't fit the prototype of complaisant young females which is expected of us," Alice said. "So we were to be given a lesson in good behaviour."

"Mm," Betty Hamilton murmured pleasantly, "Didn't they respect your upbringing by the wolves of the forest?"

Alice and Rachel both laughed. "I think they had quite forgotten the wolves," said Alice. "Would you like to come back with us and have a cup of tea. We're staying at Rachel's tonight because Alice's Mum and Dad are in London at a meeting and we've brought the dogs over. They're bull terriers as you probably know, but your lovely fellow probably knows them too."

"Indeed he does," said Jack. "Surely you remember we've taken them out ourselves on one or two occasions."

"Oh, Lord, yes," Alice cried. "I'm so sorry. I remember you perfectly now, because we've met in our house but you were wearing something else. I thought I recognised you, but it was some time ago!"

The Hamiltons looked at each other and nodded. "That is a very kind offer and would be most welcome. We know Rebecca and Joseph. In fact it wasn't all that long ago that both you and your parents came for a dinner. It might even have been a birthday treat for the pair of you."

"You probably wouldn't have seen much of either of us then," Betty added, "as we're always busy running the place during mealtimes, so we don't have all that much contact with our guests apart from complaints of course." They both smiled at the girls.

"Here we are then", said Rachel as they arrived at the door of the Old Rectory which was Rachel's home. "Hey, Mum, Dad," she called as they went in. "We've brought visitors for tea. Hope that's all right." Rebecca came out into the hallway. "Jack! Betty! How nice. Come in, my dears. You're always welcome as you know. Hullo, Roger," she greeted the dog. "Would you like to go out in the garden and play with the boys?" The girls gave Rebecca a hug and she invited her visitors into their drawing room where, to everybody's surprise, Tom and Vera were seated at the card table. They got up to greet the visitors and Alice and Rachel rushed over to give their Mum a kiss and a hug for their Dad. "I thought you were away today," Alice said.

"It all got cancelled just after you left this morning and we'd brought the dogs over and were just about to get into the taxi," Tom said. "So we decided to stay and annoy your parents instead," added Vera. "Just a special treat for the old folk, you know."

"Who's a patronising cow, then?" demanded Alice.

Tom and Vera greeted the Hamiltons and they all decided to move out into the garden for tea as the weather was warm and pleasant and just ideal for being outdoors.

"Haven't you been into the shop today?" Rachel asked Tom. "Not much point, really," he replied lazily. "I'd already booked the extra staff and Jerry manages it perfectly well. I let them know I was back in case of emergency, but it's nice to have a day off occasionally. They'll have to pay the cancellation fees anyway," he added, referring to his London handlers. "How did you two meet up with our favourite landlord and his missus?" he asked Alice.

"Well, we were having some words with some of the boys from school - in the forest - as you do - and one thing led to another - er - and- well, we all met up," Alice finished with a bright smile all round. "They were walking their dog, you see." She looked round at each of the faces in front of her in turn, but there didn't seem to be any help forthcoming from any quarter.

"Roger," she added hopefully. "Their labrador, you know. He's outside now playing with our dogs." The silence extended itself. "They seem to be getting on quite well together." There was another long pause. Everybody seemed to have stopped breathing. "I think I'll just go and check on them while you're making the tea, Mummy," she said, slightly desperately and looking straight at Rebecca. A twitch passed over Vera's face. She sent a forbidding look in Alice's direction and drew Rachel to herself. "Do you consent to this exchange of mothers, Rachel, or is this just some Machiavellian ploy by the mendacious and deceitful fruit of my loins to cover up some appalling transgression. Has your vicious little friend actually murdered one of her schoolmates? Are there corpses to be disposed of? If so, what matter?" She paused dramatically, placing the back of her uplifted arm over her brow. "How sharper than a serpent's tooth it is to have a thankless child!"

"Especially now that she has renounced her own mother," Rebecca cried theatrically. "Alas, Alack, Oh woe is me, Life is Dead! Dead! Dead! Hoy Vey, my life already!"

"The kettle's boiled," Joseph said prosaically. "Shall I make the tea?"

"Fine," said Vera in a normal voice. "Get yourselves into the garden and I'll get the sandwiches ready. Cake, Becky?"

"In the sideboard, love," Rebecca said. The rest of them trooped outside and settled down round the garden table.

"So what happened?" demanded Tom.

"Shall we wait until our Mums are here and then we'll tell you all about it. I don't know how much you saw or heard of it," Alice said to Jack and Betty. "I take it you snuck back, wondering what the boys were up to. Was that it?"

"Not entirely," Jack confessed. "You see, we actually spotted you up the tree. I mean," he amended politely, "those lads didn't see you because they weren't really looking or seeing, but you weren't entirely hidden, you know."

"Well, thanks for telling us that," Rachel said gratefully. "How *did* you spot us then? Did we make a movement?"

"When we arrived," Jack said, "they were all gathered round the tree and we could just see you peering out. I don't think we would have spotted you before that and I'm sure those lads would not have had any suspicion there was anybody there. No, your camouflage was excellent, but it wasn't meant to deceive us as well and you were very careful."

"It's a thing all RAF pilots learn which is to keep an eye on their rear view mirror at all times," Betty said somewhat irrelevantly. "I wasn't a pilot, but I learnt that trick when driving a car and every thirty seconds or so I flick a glance in my rear view mirror. I notice it when I forget, because almost invariably, if I take my eye off it for more than a minute, I've got some ass-hole trying to rear-end me. Weird, isn't it?" she laughed.

"Next time we climb a tree, Rache, would you remind me to take a mirror with me. I'm sure it will come in useful," Alice said slightly hysterically.

"Now don't be cheeky, Alice. That really is a bit OTT you know," Tom said reprovingly.

"No offence taken, Alice." Betty said pleasantly. "I'm queen of the *non sequiturs* and renowned for it, so you have my permission to be as cheeky as you like. In fact we could have a being cheeky contest if you would like."

"Let's have tea first," Tom said placatingly. "It's not wise to start Alice off or she get's over excited, and it will all end in tears and she'll get sick and we don't want projectile vomiting at the tea table do we Alice."

Alice turned to Rachel, "Do you wonder that we are the way we are?" she said plaintively. "I do apologise for our parents," she said gravely to their guests. "If I had known it was one of their bad days, I would never have invited you over."

"The truth is, we thought they were away in any case," added Rachel. "And of course, they've probably forgotten their medication."

"Naturally," Alice sounded relieved at the explanation. "That'll be it. Shall I prepare the syringes or will you, my dear."

"I think it should be me really, as you are so rough and ready and the poor things bleed so much afterwards. It's really quite distressing to watch."

"The trouble is you don't hold them down firmly enough, so it makes it all very difficult."

"I'm going to hold you down, young lady and sit on your head until tea's over if you don't belt up," said Vera, who had just come outside bearing two piled-up plates of sandwiches, followed by Rebecca with the teapot and cups and Joseph with the cake and various milk and sugar containers on a tray. The Hamiltons were quite used to this sort of banter from the parents and had not been the least put out by finding it endemic in their offspring as well. The parents were then given a blow by blow account of the whole episode and what had led up to it by the two girls. Jack and Betty then related their witnessing of the battle. They had in fact turned back immediately as they had been intrigued by the tension of the group of boys as they passed and were naturally curious about the outcome. They just caught the beginning of the girls descent from the tree and witnessed the total annihilation of the group at their hands.

"Where did you learn to fight like that?" asked Jack. "That's real street fighting of the dirtiest kind, but also very suitable for the countryside I must say."

"Well, we've always enjoyed a good fight ever since we were so high, and we get videos and things and practice the moves and all that," Rachel explained. "I mean it's a good sport, and we practice boxing and martial arts as well and keep fit, so we can move pretty quickly when we need to."

"We've got an instructor who comes along sometimes and does a workout with them," Tom said. "They're absolutely fearless, which is a mixed blessing, but at least they do have an element of common sense so they keep out of trouble and don't involve anybody else unless they are challenged and can't get out of it any other way."

"It's our version of the Way of the Warrior," Alice said. "We try to keep it flexible and we took an oath with our instructor only to use our skills for the good of others and not for gain. I don't see how it could be otherwise, but apparently there are those who abuse the power which I find difficult to imagine." She stood up and excused herself, saying she would be back in a moment. Rachel said diffidently, "She gets upset sometimes, especially after stress and has to go and unwind. I expect she'll be back soon." Rachel retreated into a world of her own while the three couples chatted of this and that until there was a lull in the conversation. Joseph returned to the events of that afternoon. "Do you think we should have a word with the school about those boys," he asked them. "If there's a lot of bullying going on, our two can't be expected to combat it all on their own. Even if they were successful and I'm sure they would get a long way towards complete success on their own, it would take away a lot of their energy which they would otherwise have used for their education. It's too much of a burden." He glanced across at his daughter whose abstracted gaze was fixed on a planet in another galaxy far, far away, (even in those days)! "Also, of course, they won't rest until they've got rid of the bullying, you know what they're like," he appealed to the other parents.

"I agree," said Tom. "I think we need to make sure that the school authorities are playing their part in this. It's their responsibility anyway. What's the situation there, Jack? We don't really know any of the history of the place except that it's supposed to have a good teaching reputation and a new Headmistress."

"Amelia Fairweather, yes. Nice woman. Been in for the odd meal, evening drink, glass of wine usually. Good taste, dresses nicely, smells nice, seems a warm-hearted decent sort. Just taken up the post this year, I think. Used to be the English teacher and joined the school about ten years ago. John Hedges was Head for yonks when I was a boy. Decent old chap. Army background. Good heart but had to put on a show of being tough with the lads like so many Army people. Not his thing really. Family were army you see. Assistant Head joined about the same time as Amelia. Good teacher but awful little martinet. Disciplinarian. Fault-finding. Don't like him. Grammar school for Boys until a few years ago when it went Independent Co-Ed. When old Hedges finally retired - Goodbye. Mr. Chips! - the Board chose Amelia instead of Roberts. Jeremiah furious. Still is by all accounts. Disciplinarian as I said. Sort of attitude that encourages bullying and favouritism. Not surprising really. Amelia will have her work cut out to change that. Imagine she needs some support. Suggest you go and have a talk with her. Ask the girls whether they're OK about spilling the beans about this afternoon and if they are you might use it as a lever. Those lads need some educating on how to treat the opposite sex. If what they said about these two is correct, those boys need to be taken in hand before they get busy being vengeful."

    Alice had just reappeared. She went over to Rachel and put her arms around her from behind. The other girl came back from whatever cosmos she had been visiting and clasped her friend's hands. Alice kissed the top of Rachel's head and the two girls then applied themselves to some more tea and pieces of cake.

    "I don't know how much you heard of Jack's account of the school, my darlings," said Rebecca, "but I think his advice is very sound. How say you we get in touch with your Headmistress and have an off-the-record conversation with her?"

    "Ring her up now," Alice said firmly. "Don't you think, Rache?"

"Absolutely," Rachel replied. "I know we made a pre-emptive attack, but it was justified. I'm damned if I'm going to be kicked around by anybody, let alone those thugs."

"Thank you, Jack," said Tom. "I reckon we owe you one for that and also for your serendipitous meeting with our girls. Shall I make a fresh pot of tea?"

"We," Betty said, "would love to stay and enjoy your company but we have a pub to run and any old tick it's going to be opening time, and if Jack is not at his post pulling pints and I am not slaving away in the kitchen within the next half hour we will not be very popular. So we must thank you for a delightful afternoon and so glad to have met with your charming and beautiful daughters again and I hope it will go well for you all."

"Push comes to shove, of course, you could go on home educating them and they can come and work for us at the Bedford any time they like. They'd get a good education there as well."

"That's for sure," Tom agreed, smiling. They said their goodbyes and collecting Roger they walked off towards their pub. Vera went to telephone Amelia Fairweather, first at her home and then finally at the school. She agreed to visit them later that evening.

****

There is no record of the discussion that the two families had with Amelia Fairweather, but it assuredly must have had a positive outcome as the headmistress of the girl's school stayed on for a late supper and drinks with the parents. The two girls retired early to Rachel's bedroom and curled up in bed together after a token shower and mouth washing. They were both exhausted and fell asleep almost immediately, but not before Alice had murmured to Rachel how pleased she was that they had insisted on having their outdoor shoes reinforced with steel toe-caps.

CHAPTER VII

School eventually recovered from the excitement of the previous week, the Battle at Giant Oak having gained much in the retelling. As the main source of the narrative had been culled from the various versions proffered by the defeated parties, who had somehow to justify their torn clothing and bruises to their scandalised parents, the version which circulated through the school and indeed the whole village was somewhat prejudiced. Jack and Betty refused to talk about what they had witnessed with the exception of a sharp correction from Jack when, in the presence of the regulars at the public bar a day later, one of the boy's fathers had expressed indignation at the girls' behaviour and claimed that they had sprayed their sons with some chemical that had weakened them so they couldn't fight back. Jack told him that if he ever repeated that calumny he, Jack and his wife, Betty, would bar him from his pub and take him to court for slander. He limited himself to saying that half a dozen big lads had set on two younger smaller girls and had the shit beaten out of them and they had got exactly what they deserved and he would be grateful if Mr. Causten senior would go home and belt the living daylights out of his rotten bullyboy son. Needless to say, Mr. Causten slammed down his pint and stormed off the premises. What transpired after that is unknown, but it was noticeable that young Will Causten presented himself as suitably contrite at his meeting with the Headmistress the following Monday morning. Amelia Fairweather had been undecided whether or not to make a public announcement that day or merely to deal with the six youths as a group in her study backed up by Jeremiah Roberts and the girls' parents. Finally she opted for confrontation with the reluctant co-operation of her Assistant Head, he having been coached and strictly instructed to be totally impartial in any judgement he thought fit to make. The boys were severely chastened after that interview and under no misapprehension of the outcome of any further misdemeanour.

The term rolled on and if there was any bullying it was either of a mild enough nature as to be virtually ineffective, or administered so clandestinely that no direct action could be taken about it It would have been very difficult, for instance, to take any steps against bullying in the family home and not really the concern of the school unless it affected a child's performance. The Head's way of dealing with any such instances was to try and engage the parents in taking a more positive attitude to the importance of homework and the involvement of the parents and siblings in its development. A difficult enough proposition when the whole purpose, as far as the parents were concerned, was to keep their brats out of the house for as long as possible.

Both Alice and Rachel were beginning to find their way eased somewhat in the matter of finding the right year for them commensurate with their actual standard of attainment. It was obvious to all the staff that they were well ahead of most pupils of their own age, so little by little they were promoted to levels more suited to their capabilities. The Headmistress may very well have declared herself to be immune from any accusations of favouritism, but her interest and support of the two girls was only too apparent to the world at large and could not to go unnoticed.

By the beginning of the following academic year they had been moved up to classes designed for fourteen-year-olds and were slowly but surely outstripping even these advanced grades. They were both quite content with their new classmates who, after some initial ragging, accepted them without any outward hostility.

Trouble, however, was simmering below the surface. Although the Battle of the Giant Oak had virtually faded from the minds of students and staff alike, there still remained an undercurrent of hostility from certain quarters. Of the original six boys who had formed the gang, the youngest of them, Michael Jones, he who had received the steel-capped toe of Rachel's foot in a very delicate area, had realigned himself out of the group and was now one of the girls' most ardent admirers. He had never met with such sympathy from an erstwhile opponent and indeed it was that rare compassion which had also endeared their first challenger, young Fletcher Arkwright, eventually to their side. He and his parents had, after some consideration, invited both girls round to have a cup of tea a week or so after that first confrontation, and finding them charming and without malice, they had become reconciled to being on friendly terms with them. Consequently the two girls had, on the whole, made many more genuine friends than enemies and been accepted on their own terms.

Events came to a head in the fourth week of the following year's Autumn term. Both girls were now twelve years old and were a little taller and a little fuller of figure than the previous year and in accordance with the natural growth patterns of all young human females.

The trouble arose mainly on account of the sudden hospitalisation of the Headmistress owing to an unsuspected attack of peritonitis which had been misdiagnosed as food-poisoning. That she survived the ordeal was more due to her own common sense in ringing the emergency services than in relying on her family doctor's prescription of milk of magnesia and bed rest. Immediate surgery was necessary and she was taken to Bristol as the local hospital did not have the necessary surgeon available at such short notice.

"So how is she?" the girls demanded of Rachel's parents when they arrived home from school that day. Rebecca told them that she had had a word with the ward nurse and that the patient had survived the surgery, but the sepsis had been quite far advanced. She was in the CCU at the moment and would not be ready for visitors for some days. Today was a Monday - (Sod's Law has it that if you're going to be in need of emergency treatment it will invariably fall on a weekend)! - the headmistress having fallen ill on the previous Saturday evening, so if she had been moved to a public ward by the end of the week they might be able to visit her over the weekend. Alice's parents were somewhere in South America, but the Katzs said they would drive over to Bristol with the girls if all was well.

Jeremiah Roberts had taken the place of his superior during her enforced absence and made the announcement of her parlous condition at assembly that morning. He had delegated his teaching schedule to a junior teacher and sat brooding in the Head's study about how he was going to take advantage of this situation which had fallen into his lap. He estimated that she would probably be in no fit condition to return to her post until the beginning of the following term. There were still ten weeks remaining of this Autumn semester, but he calculated that she might not be out of critical care for at least a week and then there would be a couple of weeks while she recovered from the operation and would be under observation for any signs of reinfection. After that, no doubt, she would be advised to have a convalescent trip to the seaside by which time it would be pointless for her to return to work until after the Christmas recess. Of course, she might recover much quicker and be back within a couple of weeks, but he thought that from what he had gathered from the hospital, that was an unlikely scenario. How then to use this blessed opportunity to redress some of the laxity and disregard for discipline and authority which the new Headmistress had inculcated in the ethos of the school? Granted, the incidents of bullying had dropped considerably, the general temper of the school was good and the pupils seemed to be attaining reasonably high standards of the curriculum. Notwithstanding these positive signs of an uplift in general well-being Jeremiah Roberts hankered after another age, where a strict adherence to formality and respect for their elders was shown in manner and intent by the pupils, and strict protocols of behaviour were adhered to. Admittedly, when he walked into the classroom, the class stood up and greeted him politely, having ceased whatever activity had been engaging them before his entrance. Somehow, this was not quite as satisfying as he would have wished. The truth was that, underlying this apparently polite behaviour on the part of the pupils, there seemed to lay a hidden and unspoken challenge in the eyes and very postures of the youngsters as he entered the classroom. It was almost as if they were daring him to stretch the bounds of his authority to the position they had been in past years. Then there had been a palpable sense of fear as he strode into the room and the whole class knew that, unless he was in a particularly good mood or absolutely no fault could be found with anybody's work that day, then there would be retribution in the form of a caning or a piece of chalk shot most accurately and hurtfully upon the transgressor. More serious infringements were dealt with by a visit to the Headmaster, and were generally a relief to the victim, as it was a well attested fact that old Hedgchog (Mr. Hedges as was)! had a bark considerably worse then his bite and usually ended up giving the perpetrator a mint humbug instead of a caning. In fact, he only administered one caning in his whole tenure as Headmaster and that was on a fifth form boy who, in a rage, had thrown a new boy onto the floor of the playground and broken his arm. John Hedges had also expelled the same young ruffian which had put paid to any further ill-treatment of new boys from that day forward.

Strangely enough, Roberts never learned the truth about the outcome of these confrontations and no one was going to enlighten him. His fond memories were of a succession of condemned malefactors having been sent home after their condign punishments at the hands of the Torquemada in the Headmaster's study. After musing his way through the first two classes of the day, Jeremiah Roberts decided he would take over his classes again after the mid-morning playground break.

Mathematics, and in particular, Quadratic Equations, were that morning's subject. "What can you tell the class about Quadratic Equations, Katz," he demanded. Rachel stood up and delivered a short and succinct account of the functions and practicality of the subject. The rest of the class kept their eyes fixed firmly on their desktops. Alice glanced up with slightly elevated eyebrows. Roberts demanded to know why she was looking so puzzled.

"The Headmistress said...." Alice began.

"Stand up when you speak to me," snapped Roberts. Alice stood up obediently.

"My apologies, sir," she said. "We were told that we would not be starting with quadratic equations until next term, sir."

"I see, well sit down, Darwin. Now, Katz, how do you happen to know so much about quadratic equations when the rest of the class has not even started to be taught this subject?"

"Mathematics is one of my interests, sir," she replied. "I have read a number of treatises on the subject."

"You would be well advised not to delve into subjects which are beyond your comprehension at your age, otherwise you will be hampered when you finally come to be properly instructed on such a subject. You are not to pursue this subject any further except under the guidance of your teacher, do you understand?"

"Absolutely, Mr. Roberts. I shall make sure that all references to quadratic equations are expunged from my home and I will personally burn all reference books on the subject, with the exception of those library books touching on the subject which I will return immediately."

There was a dead silence in the room. Roberts' eyes glinted malevolently at Rachel who placidly returned his glare.

"Make sure you do, Katz," Roberts retorted nastily. "Sit down now." He glared round the room. "So what have you been studying up until this time?" he demanded. Will Causten raised his hand.

"Please, sir," he began.

"Stand up, boy," Roberts commanded. Will stood up.

"Please sir, we had started on Trigonometry and trigonometric functions, sir, please sir."

Alice found it difficult to suppress a snigger which she deftly turned into a cough. Roberts eyed her with distaste. "Is the subject one of your hobbies as well, Darwin?" he enquired malevolently. Alice stood up.

"Not so much, sir. My interests are more literary than mathematical."

"Well, I'm sure we're all relieved to hear that, missy," the master retorted. "After all, one mathematical genius is quite enough for a class this size, I'm sure we can all agree." A sycophantic snicker went round the class, Alice sat down and had a picture in her mind of the Assistant Head Teacher stripped naked and strung out above a cauldron filled with red hot coals and a gigantic poker sticking out of his rectum which was being feverishly wielded by a grotesque goblin with a giant erection. Rachel, glancing across at her friend, saw the faint shadow of a smile flit across her sweet little face. That does not bode well for the health of this man, she thought, accurately enough!

****

"What were you thinking about after that little spat with Roberts this morning?" Rachel asked as the two girls settled down to their lunch. The weather was still fine enough for them to eat outside which they found infinitely preferable to using the communal dining-room except when it was raining. Alice described her little phantasy in detail.

"Wow!" said Rachel. "That's some imagination you have there, kiddo!"

"Comes of reading all those naughty books like Rabelais and Voltaire. The French are a bit more immediate somehow in their viciousness," she said happily.

"I do so agree," Rachel said. "You know, I think we're due for some unwelcome attention until Amelia gets back, don't you?"

"I do and I think we should go carefully. Let's not wind up the Prat too much or his spring might break and then where would we be?"

"Where indeed? Bogie approaching at your 3.0'clock." Will Causten sidled up to them.

"Pushing it a bit, weren't you/" he said to Rachel. "You should be more careful. You don't want to make an enemy of Mr. Roberts, you know. Might find yourself back in the kindergarten where you belong if you don't behave."

"I didn't start anything this morning and I think Mr. Roberts and I have a reasonable understanding between us without necessitating your intervention, thank you, Causten,"

"We are quite capable of answering for ourselves, you know," Alice said mildly. "We have no need of a mediator."

"Was I talking to you?" he demanded. "If I want your advice I'll ask you for it."

Alice turned and looked him straight in the eye. "Go away, please," she said firmly. "We are having our lunch and you are about to overstay what little welcome you've been afforded, so hop it."

In reply he reached out his hand with the intention of grabbing one of their sandwiches only to find the hand and arm to which it was attached painfully twisted in a contrary direction which forced his body into an uncomfortable position kneeling at their feet. Rachel shook her head.

"You never learn, do you?" she said sadly. "Do get it into your head that we're not to be played with or bullied and if you think you are going to get away with this sort of behaviour because the Headmistress is in hospital you've got another think coming. Now, please run along and stop all this childishness." Alice released the boy and he struggled to his feet.

"You've not heard the last of this!" was his Parthian shot.

"Probably not," Rachel said as the boy slunk off to join his friends. "Also I think the Prat saw all that and has most likely interpreted it to his own satisfaction."

"Blotted our copybooks again, have we," Alice laughed. "Oh well, in for a penny, in for a pound."

"Might as well be hung for a sheep as a lamb,"

"Better an egg today than a hen tomorrow,"

"A bird in the hand....."

"Better low than broken,"

"Takes two to Tango!"

" 'Ere 'e comes the 'oly 'umbug, 'umming 'is 'oly 'ymns to ' isself!"

"!"

"Bogey, 6 o'clock!"

"Up to your strong-arm tactics again, I notice," said a voice behind Alice.

The two girls stood up. "Just a playful little demonstration, sir," said Alice. "Causten was just enquiring how to apply the arm-lock on a miscreant and I gave him a simple demonstration. I think he was most grateful."

"He was certainly very impressed," Rachel added somewhat incautiously. Roberts eyed the two girls coldly. Without another word he turned and made off towards the school building. The girls resumed their seats and finished their lunch.

"I think, you know, that it might be a good idea to have our lunch outside the school gates in future, don't you?"

"Let's give it a go tomorrow if the weather holds," Rachel said. "Meanwhile, on with the motley!"

"Indeed," said Alice. "Thou art not a man, thou'rt but a jester!

On with the motley, and the paint, and the powder!
The people pay thee, and want their laugh, you know!
If Harlequin thy Columbine has stolen, laugh Punchinello!
The world will cry, "Bravo!" she declaimed.

"What's that from?" Rachel asked.

"Pagliacci, the opera. Good, ain't it?"

"Mm, you are clever," She gave her friend a hug.

"Not half," Alice said, hugging her back and feeling mightily pleased with herself.

"Saw that!" yelled some of the children in the playground.

"Huggy hugger, kisser kissy,
Who's a bugger, who's a sissy!" they chanted.

The two girls sprang into action and, issuing war whoops, cavorted round the playground at breakneck speed targeting the mockers and gently cuffing them with their satchels. The pandemonium subsided as the bell went for the end of the lunch break and all the children trooped back into the school flushed and exhilarated by their frolic.

CHAPTER VIII

Henry Fairweather, the Headmistress's husband was allowed to pay a short visit to his wife on the Wednesday following her admission and emergency surgical procedure which had excised the perforated appendix. He was concerned about the weakened state of his normally robust partner, but she assured him that she was now out of danger, on the mend and well on the road to recovery. She hoped to be moved from the CCU before the end of the week and was quite content not to be placed in a private ward. The close proximity of members of her own sex, grizzling and complaining, she said, would encourage her to heal faster and get as far away from the hospital as possible in the shortest space of time. Henry complimented her on her modest ambition and remarked that being at death's door had not noticeably affected her courageous spirit. She tartly replied that she would be grateful if he would cease uttering such sanctimonious tripe and bring with him on his next visit a copy of Finnegans Wake which would be an antidote to the vacuous bleating she expected to be surrounded with when she was finally moved. She also enjoined upon him a request that he would contact the two girls and their parents, whichever one was in charge at the time, and ask them to visit her as soon as the hospital permitted. He told her that Doctor Rebecca

Katz had telephoned him that very morning to ask after her and enquire when it would be possible for the family to visit.

"If I'm not out of CCU by the weekend," she said, "then Dr. Katz will have to use her professional pull to engineer a visit here. She can be my GP if necessary."

Henry, relieved at his wife's unimpaired determination and resilience, promised to telephone the family on his return and would himself return later that day with James Joyce and any news from the Katz family.

Alice and Rachel returned that day after school to an empty house as both doctors were busy at their surgery on South Street and wouldn't be home until about 6.00. Henry Fairweather telephoned the house as they were both sitting down to their tea. They promised to have one of their parents return his call immediately on their return if he did not want to speak to them at the surgery. He said he would prefer not to interrupt them at their place of work, but would like to be able to give his wife some assurance that she would be visited by the weekend at the latest. Rachel, who had answered the telephone, assured him that they were ready and willing to pay his wife a visit at the first opportunity and glad to hear that she felt well enough for visitors. She asked him to convey to the Headmistress their best wishes for a speedy recovery and said the family would be in touch later.

"Wonder what the Head's so worried about," Rachel said as she sat down at the tea table. "It must be something important enough to override her concerns about her own recovery."

"Simple enough, I would have thought, even to one of your limited intelligence," Alice said, buttering a toasted muffin. "Here, get your laughing gear round this while I toast some more of these." She sliced another couple of the articles and placed them in the toaster.

"Obviously it's to do with the school and with us and the school, otherwise she would have invited her deputy head to go and visit her, an eventuality which I cannot imagine, no how, no way."

"Precisely, Watson, so what may we deduce from that?"

"Elementary, my dear Holmes," taking a bite of muffin loaded with strawberry jam, "Something's afoot in the rotten state of Denmark."

"That would be rebellion by.....?"

"Obviously her ambitious deputy head, possibly in cahoots with certain young persons of the male sex who do not have our best interests at heart, all of whom pray and ardently wish for her and our downfall."

"This to be achieved by......?"

"Naturally, by fomenting trouble and heartache for aforesaid decent upstanding beautiful females!"

"And this is to be accomplished how.....?"

"Possibly an open challenge and contest of arms and most likely in public and involving lots of bad publicity for the hopefully defeated good guys – hopefully defeated only by the bad guys, just to avoid any confusion in your naturally limited thought processes."

"*Touché!* And what shall us good guys have in their armoury to counter this attack and come out smelling of roses, roses, roses, and none of that unpleasant shit stuff?"

"Your champion and best possible friend is at this very moment working on an idea which she cannot divulge as it is so outrageous and inspirational she is obliged to hug it to her bosom and nurture it gently until such time as it can be sprung upon a surprised and adoring world."

"I see. Well, the bosom bit is all right, and a very nice bosom it is too. I suggest that when we have finished out repast we repair upstairs and play gentle kissing games with each other's bosoms, as I for one have had enough of the outside world at the moment and want some cosseting and affectionate grooming in a warm and cosy place with my favourite lovely person. Is that agreeable?"

"It is entirely agreeable and now you mention it I feel a reciprocal need of such attention. One moment while I finish the muffin and my cup of tea and then my lips and indeed all of me will be at your service."

"I don't see why your stomach should hold precedence over my sensual needs, do you?"

"Of course they do. You don't want me leaping out of bed at some critical point and rushing down here dying of starvation and my stomach rumbling, do you. And what would happen if indeed I had this need and the door suddenly opened and there were my parents standing shocked and awed at my nakedness and flagrant disregard for decency and modest social conventions?"

"You mean you wouldn't even have stopped to put on a dressing-gown in your mad rush for sustenance?"

"Of course not, otherwise it wouldn't be a mad rush, now would it?"

"I think I shall just go upstairs and warm the bed up and perhaps play gently with myself until you care to abandon your selfish behaviour and attend to the friend who loves and adores you and has needs that only you can fulfil."

"You're about as manipulative as that bastard Roberts, aren't you?"

"So Mr. Bond, you have discovered my secret weapon, have you?"

"Yes and I know where you keep it!" So saying Rachel leapt out of her chair and chased the fleeing Alice up the stairs to her bedroom where we shall leave them to pursue their pleasures in peace.

****

Jeremiah Roberts had indeed allowed himself to be seduced into contemplating a future where he would be permanently in the position he now found himself owing to the sudden indisposition of his superior. He felt well suited to the role he was understudying at the moment and passionately wished for an extension of tenure. He contemplated a future in which several annoyances of the moment had vanished and he found it good. He did not relish or welcome the sort of opposition which presents a challenge out of which a further growth of maturity naturally takes place. He had little or no concept of obstacles being turned into stepping-stones in life's passage. Rather he wished for all and every opposition to be removed so that he could rule supreme in his miniature fiefdom. That it was the gift of the governors of the school, he was perfectly aware and indeed he had had some support for his consideration for the post that Amelia Fairweather now held. But it had not been sufficient to get him his wish as, charming though he could be when his own interests were at stake, there were enough members of the Board of Governors who saw through the mirage to the reality which drove him. Though admitting of his undoubted qualifications as a teacher, the tyrannical and cold-hearted soul was there for eyes which could see. His imagination also was lacking, as he could not contemplate that there might be other candidates for the post if the present incumbent could not continue for any reason. Even if he scored a win over her and at the same time caused the two pupils who so cleverly challenged his authority to be expelled, it would only be a Pyrrhic victory, as the majority of the Board had no intention of ever allowing him to take over the reins for any period longer than the end of the present term.

Unable to contemplate any possibility of failure in his ambitions however, he set about establishing a rapport with those pupils he thought were open to suggestions of a movement of opposition to the present regime. Iago like, he sent numerous messages of condolence to his stricken colleague, wishing her speedy recovery, assurances of loyalty and other obsequies including a casual note to the effect that he been obliged to reprimand Alice Darwin for insolence (dumb) and for an overheard remark of Rachel Katz which was disrespectful to the Headmistress herself, none of which carried any weight with her. On the contrary, it intensified her anxiety concerning his activities while she was powerless to see matters for herself. Hence her need for a consultation with the two girls who were intelligent and disciplined and would be more aware than most of the rest of the school concerning her deputy's intentions. Meanwhile her hands were tied and she had to console herself with the knowledge that however clever and manipulative Roberts was, he could not move too fast in his machinations if indeed he were planning some coup. She bided her time until the end of the week when she was moved into one of the normal wards for convalescent patients and eagerly awaited the visit from the Katzs.

Meanwhile the two girls were picking up bits of information and testing alliances amongst their fellow pupils. It was becoming clear that Jeremiah Roberts was encouraging their old enemy, Will Causten, his henchman Jumbo, and the other three members of the original gang to foment a public confrontation with the two girls and then lay the blame for the disturbance squarely at their feet. Concurrent with this plan, the teacher made life as difficult as possible for the two girls by a process of attrition which would have destroyed many a person of more mature years and experience. The pair were not to be beaten though. By the simple expedient of detachment and apparent submission to all the slights and subtle verbal assault to which they were subjected, their integrity remained solid. The knowledge that they would survive kept them serene and calm in spite of the teacher's best efforts at their humiliation. And what was the attitude of the teaching staff to this blatant abuse of their deputy headmaster's authority? Well, they chose to remain blissfully unaware and completely neutral. It wasn't that they agreed or disagreed with what was going on; they merely chose not to get involved. After all, their jobs and reputations were at stake here. If their boss decided he had an animus against these precocious children then it was obviously in their own best interest not to be so precocious and to take their medicine like any other self-respecting youngster. As they themselves never questioned this treatment or made any complaint then that absolved anyone on the staff interfering with the process. Didn't it?

However, it didn't stop the two victims sharing the news of their constant humiliation with their parents, or with a modified and played down version when relating events to their hospital visitee. They assured her that they needed no rescuing from their present predicament and that it was all fuel for the forthcoming showdown which they considered inevitable.

"What form do you think it's going to take?" Amelia asked them worriedly.

"I think one of them will issue a challenge, probably in the playground one day after school, and then there'll be a scrap and then we'll get charged with having started it somehow, then we'll get expelled and then your name will be mud for having encouraged us for getting above ourselves and we'll all go to hell in a handcart!" Alice finished breathlessly.

"Isn't that just so super?" Rachel crowed exultantly. Her parents seated round the hospital bed, the Headmistress propped up in the hospital bed, the attendant nurse standing by with her mouth open and some of the other patients and their visitors gave a great cheer and Amelia Fairweather almost broke down into tears, but whether from laughter or emotional distress wasn't quite clear.

"Oh my dears," she cried, "you really are cautions, both of you, and I do wish I could be there to witness it all! Now you will take care won't you? I don't want you getting hurt or damaged or in trouble of any sort, promise me you won't!"

"We'll do our best," Alice said soberly. "But the only way out of it would be for us to leave, and I don't really think that's on the cards, is it?"

"I totally agree with you, of course, but I'm so sorry you have this danger hanging over you both. You certainly don't deserve this vile treatment that man and those idiot boys are putting you through. If you decide not to go through with it, you know you have my support. I'll find you a better school and if necessary I'll abandon this one, but I don't want it to go down the drain. I've invested a lot of energy into its improvement and good management and I'm furious that that awful man is conspiring to bring it down." She thought for a moment. "Would it be any use of I had a word with the Governors,?" she asked them. "I'm sure it would stop this situation escalating until I can return and deal with it in person."

"Look, Headmistress, if you do it will be categorically denied, and then where would you be? Also, it might go even further underground and then burst out one day more virulent than ever."

"Like bindweed," added Rachel. "You see, we may be convinced but to an outsider it probably seems entirely inferential. There's no hard evidence of a plot, just our intuitive knowledge of who and what we're dealing with. I mean, none of this would stand up in a court of law, so the only hard evidence we'll get is the manifestation of our suspicions by an actual act of violence against us."

"We won't give up, Headmistress," Alice assured her. "We won't give up for one moment and you will soon get better and will return to us. He can't do any lasting damage and maybe, in spite of everything, some good will come of it."

"At least it will make a number of people sit up and think whether they could have made a difference," Rachel added.

As they left the hospital, Joseph, who had been very quiet during the visitation, spoke his thought out loud.

"Would you be able to know in advance where and when you expect this to take place, and do you think you could give me some advance notice of it?" They looked at him thoughtfully. "We'll let you know, darling Papa," Rachel said, taking his arm affectionately as they walked towards their car.

CHAPTER IX

The following week saw a change in the deputy head's strategy. Where before he had been aggressive and intimidating with the two girls, he now chose to ignore them more or less completely. At class he would neither single them out for a catechism nor mock them for their appearance, young age or pretentiousness. Instead he demonstrated quite subtly his sponsorship of his protégés and in particular Will Causten, coaching him privately with his studies and playing the benefactor in small matters such as turning a blind eye to certain bullying tendencies which were regaining the currency which had been forfeited when the Headmistress had been in command. If Will or any of his particular chums overstepped the bounds of acceptability in their exploits, the deputy would gently take them aside and coach them in more silent and devious ways of achieving their ends.

"It's becoming a real school for villains, ain't it?" Alice said to her circle of friends some three weeks after their first visit to the hospital. "Yeah, it's getting really bad," a large, well built girl called Anna volunteered. "Got some money pinched the other day and would that creep Roberts believe me when I told him that arsehole Peters had nicked it?" (Peters being one of the Causten gang). "Oh no, it must have been one of the girls," she mimicked, "probably that Darwin child that you're always hanging round with! That's what he said, the slimy bastard."

"How much did he pinch?" Rachel asked her.

"Five bloody quid, that's what. I'd been saving up for a prezzie for my Mum's birthday. Left me satchel with the purse inside when I was at footie the other day, came back and it had gone."

"The purse as well?"

"The whole flaming satchel. Found it outside the school gates on my way home, except for the purse."

"How did you know it was him and how did he get away with carrying your satchel off in full view?" asked one of the boys in the group.

"Good question. I noticed him squatting on the grass next to my clobber during the game. He had his coat on the ground next to him which must have been spread out over my satchel, so he just carries it off under his coat, see!"

"Yes, but," somebody started to object.

"Yes, but bollocks," Anna interrupted. "I challenged him, but he had his gang with him which is why I went to Roberts in the first place. I thought bullying was a thing of the past here. I'm really pissed off about this."

Rachel caught Alice's eye. "We'll see what we can do, but we can't guarantee a happy ending," she said.

"Why should you fight our battles for us?" Anna complained.

"Well, it's not just your battle is it?" Alice said reasonably. "It's the thin end of the wedge. Let them get away with this, then there'll be something else and Roberts will condone it because his favourites are involved. That lot are his pets at the moment because we think he's gearing them up to give us a going over and Will Causten and his gang are going to do his dirty work for him."

"So in a way, we should stick together because we want you on our side and we won't abandon you after it's all over like Roberts, sure as eggs is eggs, will abandon those boys."

"Humph! I bet you say that to all the girls," Anna said with a smile on her large face. "Yeah, well, suck it up, girl, that's the way it is," Alice said cheerfully. "I think things are coming to a head, so we might wait to recover your property until after whatever is going to happen happens, just to lull them into a false sense of superiority."

"Ho, very subtle, I'm sure," said Michael Jones, who had gained a degree of self-respect and social assurance since aligning himself with the two girls. "I believe you," he added.

"So do I really," said Anna and a murmur of approval went round the group.

"What are they going to do, do you think?" Michael asked.

"Well, if I was planning this," Rachel mused. "I'd make sure that it was public but that there was nobody present who could or would be able to stop the proceedings. I would need a captive audience and a safe arena. Here would be a good place for the showdown," she continued. "Here in the playground."

"Just like 'High Noon' with Gary Cooper as the good guy and Grace Kelly as his girl," sighed a romantic young person who had a crush on Alice.

"So which of them is Gary Cooper and which of them is Grace Kelly?" demanded Anna with a laugh.

"It's probably quite interchangeable," Rachel said smiling. "I know who the bad guys are, though," she said grimly. "Immediately you know when it's going to happen, will you all let us know, please? We've just got a few little arrangements to make."

"Nothing serious, folks," Alice chimed in chirpily. "We've already made out our wills so no problems there!"

In spite of their cheery and optimistic attitude with their friends, neither of them could shake off a feeling of trepidation. They felt that they were walking on eggshells and that at any moment they might get trapped into a situation from which they would find it hard to escape without hurt. Of the two, Alice was the most concerned for their safety. Rachel had a naturally more fatalistic outlook and did not feel the more acute vulnerability of her friend. On their way home after school that day, Alice remained sunk in low mood which was most unusual in one normally high-spirited and open-hearted. Rachel knew better than to try to jolly her out of this state and they returned to the Old Vicarage in a brooding silence.

"What's with them today?" Vera demanded crossly. She and Tom had returned the previous day from a particularly unpleasant mission involving, what was not so very usual for them, an active part in the rescue of a journalist kidnapped by a drugged up, crazed group of *soi disant* freedom fighters. (This, in practical terms, meant that they felt themselves free to shoot up on any target to which they took a disliking). The mission went very badly. The freedom fighters were completely eliminated in a very bloody exchange of fire but so was the journalist. Three of the team were badly injured and extracting them from the jungle area had proved arduous and expensive. Vera and Tom were not very happy but did their best to leave the Columbia jungle behind them. However, highly strung nerves don't vanish overnight and the atmosphere in the Katz household was still electric when the two girls arrived home.

Alice, when she heard her mother's tetchy enquiry, sat down carefully at the kitchen table.

"I know you probably don't want to be bothered with this piffling little *contretemps* we are having at school at the moment, Mum," she opened with. "And if you don't relish listening to my silly little whining voice, just let me know and I'll go and sit in the garden and tell Paddy and Jason about it. I'm sure they will be much more sympathetic." Paddy and Jason were the bull terriers belonging to the Darwins. "I realise you have both been under a lot of pressure and you have my total support for your present distress." She stopped and eyed her parents questioningly. Vera plonked herself down on the a chair facing her and Rachel sat next to her. Tom leaned against the door with his hands in his pockets and Joseph and Rebecca joined the party at the kitchen table.

"Speak, child," Vera commanded. And Alice spoke. She started by slowly and carefully narrating the happenings at her school since the Headmistress had been hospitalised. As she got into more of the details of their persecution at the hands of the Deputy Head, her delivery became less measured and the pitch of her voice rose incrementally with each injustice. Her colour which was in any case rosier than normal when she had first entered the house, gradually became suffused with more blood and as her voice rose, not only in pitch but also in decibel level, so her face became redder until Rachel, for one, feared that the blood would suddenly come shooting out of her eyes and smoke from her ears and she would perhaps burst into flames. Her choice of language became more and more colourful and words were soon flying out of her mouth which might have disgraced even a costermonger and which were certainly a surprise to both sets of parents, who wondered where she had managed to source them, quite a few of them culled from such esoteric languages as Mandarin Chinese, Indian, Arabic and European roots. The climax came with a beetroot red schoolgirl leaping to her feet, beating the table with both hands and invoking the wrath of Yahweh, Jehovah and all the gods down to Satan in a high pitched scream, the energy of which collapsed her on her back where she lay in a gigantic tantrum drumming her heels and beating her hands on the floor until, with a sudden shout, she lay very still and scarcely breathing. Rachel flew to her side and lifting her head cradled the stricken girl in her arms. Murmuring endearments and kissing her gently and repeatedly, she picked her up bodily and carried her into the living room where she sat down on the settee with Alice in her arms and crooned away softly to her. The parents all followed and knelt round the settee while laying affectionate hands on her hands and feet and gently stroking her.

"She's so hot," Rachel said quietly. "There, there, my darling, we're all here for you." She kissed her friend gently and soon Alice fell asleep in her arms.

"Look at her sweet little face," Rebecca said lovingly. "Isn't she just the loveliest child you ever did see?" Rachel raised her eyebrows at her mother.

"And aren't you the other loveliest child, too!" Rebecca added. The two grinned at each other.

"Angel face, devil heart!" Vera remarked drily.

"Never, she's the kindest, most loving person I know," Rachel defended her friend. "Bad Mumsy," she scolded Vera. "Good Mumsy," she lauded Rebecca.

"God help us!" said Vera. "I think I'll freshen up this pot of tea," she volunteered. "Or shall I make a fresh brew?" Without waiting for an answer she made for the kitchen and busied herself with cups and saucers. Without a word, Tom put up the card table and arranged four chairs around it. Vera came back into the living room with a laden tray.

"Tea," she said succinctly. She poured out a mug for Rachel and herself and left the others to help themselves. The adults settled down to a hand of bridge, Tom partnering Rebecca and

Joseph partnering Vera. Rachel remained on the settee cradling Alice who had turned her back on the room and was now laying with her head on Rachel's lap. Some time later she stirred and sat up. The adults stopped their game to turn and look at her. Rachel got up and poured her a mug of tea. She mouthed a thank you and took a sip .

"How are you feeling now,?" Tom asked her. She thought for a moment.

"I feel," she began slowly, "as if I have just been reborn. I feel so alive and at peace that I can't quite believe it. What happened exactly?"

"You don't remember?" Vera said incredulously.

"I don't remember anything since I started telling you about what had happened at school while you were away. Then it became confused and I wasn't anywhere any more, just a sort of blinding light and a lot of noise. I could hear somebody screaming. Was that actually me?"

"Yes, my dear, that was actually you," Rachel said amusedly. "It was quite a performance."

Alice looked thoughtful. "I completely lost it, didn't I?" she admitted.

"Completely," agreed Rachel.

"I think I must go to bed and sleep now." She got up slowly placing the empty mug back on the tea tray. She turned to Rachel and hugged her. "Will you come up soon?" she pleaded.

"Of course, sweetie," Rachel said fondly. Alice went round the assembled parents hugging them all in turn. "I do so love all of you," she said simply and disappeared upstairs. There was a reflective silence. Then Tom spoke.

"Well, I think that was probably one of the best homecomings we've ever had, don't you ducks," he looked at Vera.

"Can't fault it really," she chuckled. "But now I think I would like to have a less dramatic rundown on what has been going on at your school, Rachel, if you would be so good as to let us in on the drama."

"How about we continue this game a bit later and we all sit down for dinner now," said Rebecca. "I for one am in need of sustenance and Jerry will be in soon wanting his supper, so Rachel can bring us up to date and Joseph and I can fill in one or two gaps in the tale as well."

"I shall go upstairs and see if our little angel needs anything and then I will come down and tell all," Rachel said, and disappeared upstairs. She returned a few minutes later.

"She's fast asleep and Paddy and Jason are upstairs looking after her so she's happy and content and safe as houses."

Jerry had just come in and Tom was giving him a short version of what had transpired that afternoon.

"Wow!" he said, with an amused expression on his face. "Did she have a rebirth then?"

"What's that when it's at home?" Tom demanded.

"All the go, nowadays, with the New Age lot. Rebirthing. Encounter groups, all that sort of thing." He laughed. "Got to keep up with the times, you know!"

"No, we don't," Vera contradicted him. "We're not obliged to keep up with anything, but feel free if you want to waste your time and money on all this New Age crap."

"Don't be silly, Vera, some of the things they do are very good. I've been on one or two of these weekend courses and you get some very clever guys working them. You'd be surprised."

"No doubt," Vera said drily. "Very surprised indeed, I'm sure. Now Rachel, tell all," she commanded. Rachel told all.

"So the only thing we're not sure about is when this thing, whatever it is, this confrontation is going to take place, is that right?" Joseph asked.

"Just about," Rachel replied. "We don't know for certain, but I'm pretty sure it will be in the school playground and at a guess I would think it would be either on a Friday evening or Saturday and possibly before the half-term break which is in a couple of weeks. We've got our spies out because we reckon invitations will be issued at least not later than lunchtime the same day. What were you planning to do, Dad?" she asked Joseph.

"Oh, I thought that if we could secrete ourselves in one of the classrooms overlooking the playground, I could film it from there without any of the principals knowing about it. I will have to move fast though, obviously, as there won't be much time for preparation on the day, so could you find a good vantage point for me and a way to sneak me onto the premises at the last moment?"

Rachel looked a bit worried by this suggestion. "You know," she said carefully, "You might not want this to be recorded. I can't tell you why, because at the present moment I'm not sure what's going to happen, but if what happens does actually happen, you might be - um - sort of upset by it, I just don't know." She fell silent.

"You can't tell us what is in your mind, Rachel? And why not?" her mother asked her seriously.

Rachel fidgeted with her cutlery and avoided looking into anyone's eyes "I haven't really formulated how I'm going to deal with this situation, because I don't know how the situation is going to develop, but I do have a plan if it goes a certain way, otherwise we - I - we react as usual."

"Which is?" Tom queried.

"Oh, just kicking butt as well as we can," Rachel replied. "Look, I'm sorry, but I really cannot talk about this any more. If I give you any indication of what I have in mind if a certain situation arises, I know that you will try and talk me out of it and that will undermine my already shaky resolution and I know I won't be able to go through with it even if I wanted to and that would destroy my self confidence in any ability I have to deal with situations in a way that satisfies me. And," she added hurriedly, "it's no good asking Alice what my putative intentions are because I haven't even told her and she has absolutely no idea what is in my mind which is probably the first and last time that that has occurred between us or will ever occur again. Sorry, but there it is." she finished flatly.

"All right, my dear, we will respect that. Do you not want me to record this happening then? Would you indeed prefer that we stayed away?"

"No, of course not, Daddy, but I just don't want you to be ashamed of me. I have a lot of stuff bottled up in me, the sort of stuff that Alice has just successfully unloaded but my catharsis or lustration might be a better term, if it happens then will be just as satisfying to me as Alice's has been tonight. In fact I'm sure she will be much better prepared to meet the challenge than I am."

"Such an old head on young shoulders," Joseph smiled at his daughter. "We're very proud of both of you, you know, and I'm sure you will never do anything to disgrace either yourselves or us, so have confidence in yourself and keep schtum about your intentions. I think that is a very wise decision."

"I totally agree," Tom said. "Go for it, girl. You have our total support as always,"

The parents smiled at Rachel and she suddenly blushed and clapped her hands and laughed joyously. "Yes," she cried. "It's all going to go awfully well!"

"Right," said Vera. "We are going to thank you for a delightful supper and for looking after our girls whilst we've been on our diplomatic visit of goodwill and peace to all men wherever they may be. We are both in need of rest so we will be off with our canine friends and look forward to having you, Rachel to stay. When will you be arriving?"

"Would Monday be all right? You would probably like to have a few days rest before we descend on you."

"It's no hardship, I assure you," Tom said. "We love it when either or both of you are staying, so you really don't think you're a nuisance, do you?" he pleaded.

"I think you need a rest," Joseph said diplomatically. "So why don't you come over tomorrow night as well and that would save you the bother of having to cook so we might even go out for dinner. It's been a while since we went down to the Bedford and Betty always has something tasty on the menu."

"That's a lovely idea," Vera enthused. "We need a bit of a jolly time. Shall we meet you down there about 7.00? With the girls?"

And so it was agreed and Tom and Vera called the dogs down from the girls' bedroom and they walked back to their own house which lay about a mile away through the forest. Rachel kissed them both goodbye and went to check on her friend who was still sleeping soundly.

Some two hours later, Alice came downstairs in search of food. Rebecca and Joseph had long since retired, but Rachel was curled up with a book showing and describing aikido stances and strikes. Alice found the remains of some stew in the fridge and was eating it straight out of the pot.

"We need to up our training schedule," Rachel remarked. "Let's have a ten mile run tomorrow first thing before school. We could start off towards the farm and then do the circle round Copley woods and be back well in time for breakfast and a shower before school."

"OK," Alice said. "And we could do some target practice on the way and after school, shall we use the gym and do some boxing? They've got all the kit there and I'm sure Miss Martin would be agreeable. She'd also keep it off the record." Anne Martin was their gym instructress and boxing coach, also a favourite with the girls. "If we leave early enough, we can visit the ponies as well. We haven't been to the stables since last weekend – they'll be pining and cross if we leave it much longer.." Rachel closed her book.

"Good thinking, Batfiend! Let's get to bed this very moment and away with dull care, for tomorrow is the day of our content and England shall smile once more on deeds of valour and glory!"

"Too right, Batshit, have at them!" And they both went quietly upstairs, first turning off all the lights like good little housekeepers and making sure that the premises were well secured. "After all, we don't want to be murdered in our beds before we've had the chance of kicking the shit out of those turds, do we?" Alice said reasonably.

"Well no, indeed we don't," Rachel replied thoughtfully. "The only thing is, how do you manage to kick the shit out of a turd?"

CHAPTER X

Tom managed to persuade Harry, his personal fight trainer to spend a couple of days giving the girls some advanced training at the end of the following week. They had been disciplining themselves as well as they could on their own, but they needed the extra stimulus of a teacher to ground them in as many of a variety of defensive moves as possible. They would be coming up against young boys who were older, heavier and well motivated. If they got embroiled in too furious an onslaught involving close contact fighting, they might very well be overpowered. Skill at avoiding such a contingency was paramount as was the ability to deflect any blow with or without a weapon. Disarming a knife-wielding youth, even one who was not over-skilled, had its obvious dangers. It was only too easy for a knife to find its way past a defensive blocking arm and into a vital organ which would be a disaster. It was unlikely that any of the gang would be equipped with such a weapon, but the unlikely had to be catered for. "If I'm there and I see any evidence of a knife appearing in any of those boy's hands, I'll put a bullet in his head," Tom declared. "And I'll put a bullet somewhere else which won't please him either," Vera said grimly.

The trainer had a bit more confidence in his pupils. "They're both like lightning," he assured the parents. "And they're also very sensible. They'll run, if one of them tries anything like that and they can run like the clappers."

"They can't run anywhere if they're surrounded by a mob of screaming school kids," Vera said. "This is going to take place in an arena. They won't want to run, even if they could, so we need to be confident that it's going to be a fair fight. I don't trust those boys. They might even be doped up for all we know. It happened once before and the girls were only three years old then!" She related the story of the nursery school attack to the trainer. "Also, we've just had to deal with a bunch of doped up killers, and it's no laughing matter, so forgive us if we're a bit touchy about the subject."

Harry called the girls over from where they had been having a rest.

"Let's give your parents a little demo, shall we?" he said. They were in the garden at the Darwin's house. "Fetch me a wooden spatula or something wooden resembling a knife from the kitchen, would you please," he said. Alice ran into the kitchen and came back with small wooden serving spoon.

"Excellent," he said. "Now, you first, Rachel." And with that he turned on Alice and lunged at her with the handle of the spoon. His attack was very professional with an upper thrust from below his waist. Alice twisted her body round and locking his active arm between her right arm and her body she brought him to the ground by pushing his shoulder blade from behind with her left hand. He had dropped the simulated weapon in the process.

"You see, my right arm would most likely have been dislocated," he said as got up, "but she knew not to follow through further or she would have been a trainer short this afternoon." He laughed and picking up the spoon made as if to go towards her parents who had been very impressed by this example of their daughter's prowess. Without the slightest warning he leapt at Rachel making a backward strike with his left hand. Rachel got his arm in a lock and continuing the arm's trajectory threw him on his face at the same delivering a gentle blow to the back of his neck.

"See," he said, getting to his feet again. "See what they do to me, and they actually quite like me." He grinned. "Well, I thought they did, anyway."

"Of course we like you Harry," they chorused. "Everybody likes you!"

"Look," he said to them all. "Life's a gamble, but you've got everything going for you and you're survivors, let's face it, you're survivors."

The Darwins smiled at him. "Yeah, OK," Tom said. "I reckon they can handle any of those types with or without knives."

"Let's hope none of them brings out a knife," Harry said. "It would go down very badly with them even if nobody got hurt and if they did, they would be facing a gaol sentence, that's for sure." The training continued until that evening, which was a Sunday, and the family gave him some tea and he went off quite pleased to have earned a healthy fee with free board and lodging for a couple of days with people he enjoyed being with. He had known Tom and Vera for some years, but had never had an opportunity of coaching the children before. He was very impressed with them and said so to Tom and Vera as he got into his car.

"Those two are exceptional," he said to them in confidence. "I've never had brighter or fitter or more natural talents than those girls. They've obviously been into the fight game for some time."

"They came out of the womb fighting each other," Vera said drily. "Born within two days of each other in the same hospital ward. That's where Rachel's mother and I met and became friends. They make quite a team, don't they?"

"Not half!" Harry laughed. "Well, drop me a postcard when it all kicks off. My money's on them."

Tom and Vera waved their friend farewell, and felt somewhat relieved. They had been very impressed with the girls' performance that afternoon. "He wasn't holding back, was he?" Vera said.

"Nope. That was the genuine article. Harry always delivers that and he rarely compliments anybody, so this was exceptional."

****

Amelia Fairweather meanwhile had been gradually recovering her strength and after a week of the Ilfracombe seafront grew impatient with herself and the locality and returned unnoticed to her home, arriving there at mid-day. Henry, of course, was at his bank, engaged with looking after his customers. It was in the days when banks had personal managers who were available to the general public and many years before things started to go wrong with the system. She telephoned the Darwin household to no avail, then the Katz household, also to no avail as it was a Tuesday and both couples were at work. She made herself some lunch and then had a short nap. She wanted to be up when Henry returned for his tea so as not to alarm him by being in bed when he opened the front door. Four o'clock came and she heard the door open as Henry came into the house. She called out his name and he came into the kitchen looking quite surprised.

"Why didn't you ring me at the bank?" he said. "Have you been back long?"

"No, I got in about twelve and made some soup for myself. How are you, my dear?" They kissed.

"Fine," he replied, "but why didn't you ring?"

"I didn't want anybody to know that I was back until I'd found out what was happening at the school, you see. That Mavis Fletcher would have had it all over the village in no time that I was back and that I was wearing my grey suit and hat with the feather in the rim and my brown shoes and looking frightfully pale and fragile and I shouldn't have come back so soon as the school was doing ever so well with that nice Mr Roberts and I would go and let all those children run around to do what they liked with no supervision and what was the world coming to it would never have done in her day. You know full well what a silly old cat she is, Henry."

"I get that, yes, but she is quite a good secretary all the same and at least knows her business which is more than can be said of nice little Miss Templeton who will no doubt be someone's treasure one day, but whose typewriting skills leave something to be desired."

"Henry," Amelia said firmly. "I need to get in touch with those girls and their parents at the first opportunity, and I would like to do it without anybody in the village knowing about it. In fact, I would like it to be known that I am still convalescing in Ilfracombe, so it is imperative that I am not spotted. How is that to be achieved and also how can I be here without anybody spying on me?"

"How did you get back without anybody seeing you in the first place?"

"Very expensively, I'm sorry to say, Henry. I hired a car with shaded windows and had him drop me at the top of the lane by the side of our house. I came through the kitchen door and I'm sure nobody saw me."

"Well, I shall have a cup of tea and a bun, then I shall go down to the garden centre to have a quiet word with Tom Darwin, or his brother if he's not there, and we'll arrange for one of the girl's parents to put you up for a few days which will be better for you than here because you will at least have some decent company some of the time and I'm sure they'll be happy to have you and you can plot and plan to your heart's content." Amelia embraced her husband.

"You are a clever old thing, aren't you and so devious! My dear, I would never have expected deviousness from a bank manager, I really wouldn't. A headmistress perhaps, but a bank manager? Never!"

"You really haven't had much real life experience, have you Amelia?" Henry said mournfully.

****

Transferring Amelia to the safer haven of the Old Rectory was accomplished with little fuss by Jerry driving the market garden's pick-up truck. Dressed in green overalls, a floppy hat and Ray-Ban glasses, she was smuggled on board within the hour and installed in the Katz's house even before their return from their surgery. Jerry had called in on his way to borrow the house key from Rebecca and helped Amelia to pack some extra clothing and books into her suitcase.

"How will you account for your passenger?" she asked him as they drove towards the Katz homestead.

"I won't," Jerry replied amusedly. "Anybody I don't like questions me, I'll just advise them to mind their own effing business or I'll poke them in the eye." He laughed. "That usually puts them off."

Amelia smiled happily. "Oh, I'm so glad to be back home," she said. "Ilfracombe's all right, but dear God, aren't most of those seaside towns the bitter end! I thought I would collapse from sheer boredom if nothing else. Finnegan's Wake proved to be less of a consolation than I had hoped."

"Well yes," Jerry said sympathetically. "My last choice for holiday reading unless leavened by a good alternative of Ian Fleming, Ngaio Marsh or Dorothy Sayers I would have thought."

"I'll know better next time," she replied.

"Why? Are you thinking of having some more surgery done in the near future, or perhaps you will need to go into hiding after the forthcoming shemozzle?"

"Neither, young man," Amelia rebuked him sternly. "I intend to ride high on my distress at the treacherous behaviour of my Assistant Headmaster and the undisciplined criminality of a small number of pupils which has been fomented by the former in my absence."

"That's the spirit, girl," encouraged Jerry. "Sock it to them!"

"Which is why I don't want it known that I am back in the village, you see." Jerry was silent until they drew up at the door of the Old Rectory. He got out of the car and unlocking the kitchen door, helped his passenger into the kitchen with her suitcase.

"You don't, I imagine, want it to be known that you had any complicity in whatever devilish scheme you are planning with my brother and his extended family? No accusations of acting the *agent provocateur* mayhap?"

"How right you are, Mr Darwin. Are you going to take part in these festivities?"

"I think I will content myself with a watching brief, if you don't mind, Headmistress," he said as Amelia divested herself of the overalls, floppy hat and Ray-Bans which he took from her and packed into a plastic bag. "I find that adventures featuring your two young female charges are exciting enough but when in collaboration with the parents they become positively life-threatening."

"Oh, dear, do you think I am going to be in any danger, then," she asked in mock seriousness.

"Not if you keep your head well below the parapet," he replied in kind.

"That is exactly what I planned to do in any case," she assured him. "In this sort of war-zone I am not front line material."

"More at the planning stage, as it were?" he enquired politely.

"Precisely," she said. "GHQ, back room boffins sort of thing!"

"Wacko!" said Jerry. They smiled at each other. "I'd better get back otherwise awkward questions might be trembling on scurrilous lips."

"Nicely expressed, Mr. Darwin and may I thank you most sincerely for your assistance in my predicament."

"A pleasure doing business with you, madam," he said. "That husband of yours is a real corker, isn't he? It was all his idea you know."

"I am discovering some disturbing things about my husband of which I had never had the slightest inkling. Better late than never, I suppose."

"Don't open the door to anybody," Jerry warned as he left. "They've got spies everywhere!"

"Oh my!" She shut the door on him with a smile, which faded as she seriously considered her options concerning the threatened disturbance at her school. On the one hand, the simple solution would have been to announce her return, walk into the school the very next day and take over command again, squashing any further playground challenges or undermining of her authority by the egregious Jeremiah Roberts. That should have been a simple enough choice. Roberts would be put in his place, Will Causten's little gang would have their claws clipped and the girls would be restored to honour and safety. The stumbling block, if it could so be described, was the complex character of Amelia Fairweather herself. By itself this could have remained buried in the recesses of her very soul, but for the fact that on a very deep level she responded to both Rachel and Alice's need for revenge and the sort of high drama that inspired the plays of the Jacobean stage. This was a commonality shared by the girls' parents but which their elders had come to terms with from bitter experience as not worth the candle. The time was not far off when the two youngsters would truly adopt the way of the warrior which was to settle for peace as the best outcome, but that time was not yet and they secretly lusted for a showdown and for the vanquishing of their foes.

To give her credit, Amelia Fairweather was totally honest with her hosts and Alice's parents that evening when they sat round the kitchen table to discuss the situation.

"What is the problem, then?" Joseph asked her. "Would that not be the best solution in any case? The alternative seems to be a confrontation in which somebody or more than one person may get hurt, perhaps badly. Surely you have a responsibility to avoid that at all costs?"

"What do you two think?" Tom asked the girls. Alice thought a moment while Rachel stared stonily in front of her. "It's obviously the only sensible solution," she said slowly. "The only problem that I can see, is that it may have gone too far already, and nothing you say or do will change their minds about issuing a challenge. Even though we would abide by your ruling, they will get us in a corner sooner or later and how will you be able to stop that happening?"

"It might be worth a try," Rebecca said. "See what sort of response you get." Rachel sat up in her chair.

"Mr. Roberts will first of all ridicule any collusion with any of the gang and will put it around that since your hospitalisation you have become paranoid about your authority which he will imply is on the rocks in any case. He will spread it around that you have got some unnatural feelings for us, that you are in the throes of a mid-life crisis and are suffering from some sort of sexual frustration as you have no children of your own or some such nonsense which is only too possible to gain credence with the unsophisticated and credulous inhabitants of this village. I think it would be a good idea for you to turn up unexpectedly tomorrow and just continue as normal. Don't let on that you have any suspicions about his plans for a *coup d'etat* or his involvement with Will Causten. We will keep our ears to the ground and I think the likeliest time they will strike will be this Friday after school."

"Why on earth would he sanction such an action, child, and so soon at that?" exclaimed the headmistress. "That seems so illogical."

"Forgive me, Headmistress," Alice said. "but it is only too logical. He is going to react in one of two ways to your sudden reappearance or maybe a mixture of the two. First off, he's going to panic which will throw him off centre. Then, after he's calmed down a bit he will realise this is the golden opportunity he's been waiting for. It will demonstrate that no sooner are you back in harness than all hell breaks loose and you have completely lost control of school discipline. Nothing like this happened when he was in charge, but immediately you return, chaos! Also," she added, "the sooner it happens after your return the better for him.

If he leaves it too long, you will really have got in control again and the fight may well have gone out of the boys by then."

Amelia looked stricken. "Oh my God," she cried. "You are so right. What can I do? If I don't turn up he'll take over, if I do he'll take over and whichever way you two will suffer."

"Firstly," Rachel said stoutly. "Whether or not you don't turn up again is irrelevant, the Governors would appoint a new Head, not him, I'm sure of it. We can fight our own battles. If we lose we'll go elsewhere for our schooling. It wouldn't be the same without you anyway. If we have a showdown quickly, we'll make sure that the authorities know who was behind it. One thing I'm pretty sure of and that is that Jeremiah Roberts will leave early on the day the metaphorical balloon goes up and that we will nail those boys. We have a lot of support and many good friends who will stand by us."

"Headmistress, you know we're on your side, don't you?" Alice pleaded. "You will be there with the telephone at hand in case of emergency and we will let you know when we think it's going to happen. The main thing is to convince him and everybody else that you have no suspicion of any shady business going on. He will think he has the upper hand, which is our strength and his weakness. If he suspects that you're playing a game with him, he will try another way and we may not be so successful about getting any knowledge until it's too late."

"You've been studying Wang Chen's Tao of War, haven't you," Tom said admiringly.

"That and Sun-tzu's Art of War," Alice replied modestly. "Very inspiring books."

"Indeed," Tom addressed Amelia. "Have faith in our children, Headmistress. I don't think you will go far wrong if you let them handle this. They've been getting the feel of events while you've been away and they are the people on the ground as it were.

I hope we'll be able to join you if you intend to monitor the proceedings from your study or somewhere secure."

"I hope we're right about the location," Rachel said. "I can't think where else they would set up a semi-public confrontation like this. I mean, the reason they would have it on Friday instead of Saturday is that they won't want any outside interference or witnesses."

"That's probably the truth of it," Vera remarked. "And now, let's relax and have some dinner. I've brought over a big hotpot of goodies for us all which is bubbling away merrily in the Katz Aga so let's to it!"

The meeting broke up and Amelia began to feel some hope that things were going to turn out much better than she had thought possible at the start of the evening. She also decided that it would be politic to return to her husband that very evening. Tom said he would discreetly drop her at her house on their way home. The girls, he said, were staying at the Old Rectory this week. Amelia telephoned her husband to let him know she would be returning that evening.

CHAPTER XI

The next day, Jeremiah Roberts had the shock of his life when he opened the Head's study door to find Amelia Fairweather seated at her desk and greeting him with a beaming smile.

"Jeremiah," she boomed. Roberts looked totally bewildered. "I'm now fully recovered and glad to be back in harness. I can only thank you for having held the fort so professionally whilst I was *hors de combat* as it were, what?" A thought crossed her mind that she might just be overplaying the *bonhomie*, but she ploughed on regardless. "And how have things been going on since I've been away? Any problems? Well," she continued without waiting for an answer. "I'm sure you've dealt with any little *contretemps* with your usual discreet efficiency."

"Indeed I have, Headmistress," he replied, preening himself at her generous encomium in spite of his covert hostility. "Happily, we have had no problems of any note. As you are aware, I always run a very tight ship." More like a prison ship, she amended to herself. She beamed and boomed again. "Most excellent," she cried. "Well, you just carry on. I've got some catching up to do, so I'll leave you in charge of the teaching roster today and maybe until the end of the week, while I get steadily back into harness."

"Oh, I do hope you'll feel up to taking over again by tomorrow, Headmistress," he said slyly. "I and the rest of the staff have so missed your firm hand on the tiller." So that's his game, she thought. That young Katz girl has got it absolutely right and so has Alice Darwin. Those two have his measure sure enough, and they're much cleverer at this game than I am, so I am in good hands. I can't wait to see what happens on Friday night. The absurd thought that Friday Night was Music Night came unbidden to her mind and made her smile.

"Do you find something amusing in what I have just said, Headmistress?" he enquired suspiciously.

"Heavens no," she assured him. "I was just smiling at the nourishing thought of how fortunate I am to have such a loyal second in command and such a supportive staff. Thank you again, Mr. Roberts, Jeremiah I should say. I shall look forward to taking up the reins once again tomorrow. Today though, I really need the time to reacquaint myself with my duties and also my teaching schedule and make sure I am well prepared to resume taking my classes. Ah, that was the assembly bell, was it not. I shall just say a few words to the school concerning my sudden absence three and half weeks ago. It will only take a minute, then I will hand the baton over to you to continue the day and make any announcements you may wish to make."

She beamed at him again, feeling as she did so that her career as an actor was severely limited and wishing she could just punch his lights out there and then. A different type of man than the self-serving and egotistical person before her would have doubted the mysterious change in her attitude towards him, but Roberts was content to let the shallow praises gently massage his inner being, so that he was almost purring like a contented tabby as they ascended the short flight of stirs onto the stage in the assembly hall.

"He looks almost happy," Alice murmured to her friend as they watched the pair settle into their chairs on the stage with the other teachers. "I expect she's soft-soaped him, given him a good ego massage." Rachel whispered back.

The tradition was to sing a hymn accompanied on the piano by one of the teachers, then recite the Lord's Prayer at the very beginning of Assembly. There would then be a short statement of important matters to be addressed followed by any announcements that the staff wished to make. That day the only statements were from the Deputy Head who welcomed the Headmistress back. She then gave a brief account about her stay in hospital and convalescence and the school was dismissed to their classrooms and the daily routine commenced.

Confirmation of their suspicions concerning the day and proposed venue for the forthcoming battle of the playground came at lunchtime on the Friday as Rachel had predicted. The school buzzed with excitement that afternoon and most of the teachers found their charges to be exceptionally distracted. Not having been let in on the reason for such a deficiency of attention they packed up their things at the end of the final classes and left the building relieved to be shot of such an unsatisfactory afternoon's work. The janitor had been given leave by Roberts to take the rest of the day off as he had been told that a number of pupils were staying behind for extra studies and it was uncertain how late they would be. He assured the man that he would lock up after the last pupil had left and that he, the janitor, would find the school in good order when he arrived the following morning. This suited the man as he did not live on the premises and was pleased enough to have a free early evening. The Headmistress informed her Deputy that she would be leaving the school herself shortly, as she felt somewhat tired at the end of her first week back and was content to let him see the children off the premises when he himself left.

She accordingly locked up her study and made her way ostentatiously homewards. Out of sight of the school gates, she rounded a corner into West Street, the main thoroughfare of the village, and after a short stop at the police station entered the local tea-shop where she found the girls' parents waiting for her. Joseph had a bulky hold-all beside his chair.

"My cine camera," he explained as the men stood politely to welcome her. Half an hour and several cups of tea later, they were joined by a small boy.

"Would you like a cup of tea, Timmy?" the Headmistress asked him politely.

"Please miss, I think you had better come back quickly now as Mr. Roberts has just driven off in his motor car and all the kids are milling round the playground, miss."

"Right, come along everybody. You run along, Timmy, but you can go home if you wish."

"Oh no, miss. I want to see what happens. I bet Alice and Rachel beat them, don't you?" He jigged up and down in his excitement.

"I sincerely hope so, Timmy. Now, run along do, there's a good boy."

She led her party round to the back gate of the school which was being guarded by Anna, the girls' large friend.

"Here you are, miss. I've propped open the door so you can get into your study without being seen from the playground, but best be quick. I think it's all about to kick off any moment." When they reached her study on the upper floor of the old building and cautiously peered through the window, they saw that indeed the school had surrounded the combatants in the playground below. Joseph hastily erected his camera stand with Tom's help and he focused the instrument onto the scene. "I've got a slightly wide angle lens inserted so the focus should remain constant without too much moving around. Also the window is open and I'll get some good sound - hopefully." The babble of children's voices was clear in the room. Causten and his supporters were standing in a group to the right of the study window in more or less the centre of the playground. Alice and Rachel had just emerged from the building and were making their way to the centre of the arena formed by the rest of the school. They both looked extremely neat and well turned out as usual. Their shirts had been well ironed, their blazers and skirts clean and freshly pressed, their hands and faces scrubbed and shining with health. They also looked rather diminutive and mild mannered compared to the roughness and hostility displayed by the boys facing them.

"You'll have to give us a bit more room, you know," Alice said to their audience. "We don't want anybody to get hurt who is not directly involved. In fact we would prefer that nobody got hurt. So what do you say to shaking hands and calling it a day?" she said to Causten.

"Trust you to try and weasel out of your punishment," he replied contemptuously. "You can't ambush us from a tree this time, can you?" Alice looked at Rachel.

"Let me lead this," she said softly to her friend. Alice stepped back a pace and Rachel took a casual step forward.

"Will Causten," she said firmly. "You and your friends are bullies and cowards. We do not expect any quarter from you and we will give none in return. The last time we had a confrontation, there were six of you and two of us. Now there are still five of you. I think we would have been entitled to some handicap on your part to even the odds a bit, don't you?"

"No, I don't," he almost spat at her. "This isn't some sort of jolly little sparring match between equals, this is the weight of justice coming down on your perverted and vile heads. You are perverts and you deserve to be banished from society, so we feel justified in teaching you a lesson which you won't forget."

"I see," Rachel replied calmly. "And you are acting on whose authority?"

"Our own authority, that demands decent manners and not the obscene behaviour of two twisted females."

"My, my, what integrity you claim, to be sure. Now in answer to your charge, I am only going to make one statement and that is that you have no real knowledge of our relationship and that relationship is very private and we do not display any untoward behaviour in school or out of school. In any case there is nothing unnatural about same sex relationships. They happen in all of the animal kingdom which you should know, all of you, and should not be an offence against any God or society, even though such relationships are still unfortunately demonised in some countries including the society in which we live. We make no apologies for ourselves or any like us. You, in fact, are being incited to do us violence for the benefit of someone who should know better and who will gain nothing but censure for his actions."

"What, you two girlies think you can take us on?" He laughed scornfully. "Go on then, do your best. I suppose you're loaded with secret weapons and think that you'll score points with us that way. Well, just you try it. You and your steel-capped shoes and the stones in your pocket. Bet you couldn't even hit me from this distance!" Rachel slowly took a small pebble from her pocket. She looked round for a target.

"You see that metal pole over there?" she said. It was attached to the wall which was about forty feet from where she was standing. Heads turned to look at it and with a flick of her arm and wrist she sent the pebble flying to hit the pole and shatter itself on impact. A sigh went through the assembled schoolchildren. "That's my baby," Rebecca muttered to herself from the seclusion of their lookout.

"As far as the steel-capped toes and the two of us are concerned, I am offering myself as your only opponent. If I fail, my friend Alice will challenge you. Furthermore," she held up her hand as a gasp went round the spectators. "I will remove my steel-capped shoes and other aids which you may consider an unfair advantage over the five of you." Nobody spoke as she went over to Alice and took off her blazer. Alice held out her arms to receive it. She then, standing rock still on one foot and then the other, divested herself of her shoes and socks. That done she took off her blouse, folded it and placed it on top of the blazer, then removed her skirt, undervest and knickers until she stood naked in front of the crowd. She walked back to her original position to face a now highly alarmed schoolboy. It was noticed that her feet did not just place themselves in front of her but appeared to clutch the very ground she walked on so that she seemed to be moving, as on a treadmill, the very ground beneath her. She stopped and faced him squarely.

"Before we start," she began. "I should like to make a short statement." As everybody seemed to have stopped breathing and nobody moved a muscle, she continued.

"My ancestors were Ashkenazi Jews from Russia," she announced in an unemotional voice. "After several pogroms they were hounded out of their adopted homeland and eventually turned up in Poland. Not the best place for Jews in the 1930s. When the German Nazis invaded Poland and rounded up all the Jews for the gas chambers, they first took away all their possessions, their house, their money, their animals, their loved ones, the gold in their teeth and finally the last remnants of their clothing and any sense of themselves as human beings. They then paraded them in front of the subdued populace and condemned the men to beat each other to death with iron poles and the women to trot around displaying their beautiful bodies to the jeering SS men who were going to turn those beautiful bodies into bars of soap and other useful products for the benefit of the Third Reich and their supporters." She stopped and her cool eyes surveyed the collected children with compassion. Both parents were silently crying in the Headmistress's study and Amelia herself was openly sobbing. Joseph wiped his eyes and concentrated hard on recording the scene as well as he could. Rachel could see that many of the children were in tears. "Both my grandparents had reached the safety of England at the beginning of 1935 as they had had enough of running and it was either Britain or America where they and others like them would find refuge. Their children therefore became my parents, who repay their salvation with every ounce of their energy at their disposal for the good and well-being of the people of this country. I am also grateful for being here and I will defend my right to live and be in a society free of the prejudice and blind stupidity with which I am confronted today." She looked Will Causten straight in the eyes. Unable to move and hypnotised by the icy coldness in his opponent's face he stood as if paralysed. Not so, however, his lieutenant, who uttering a defiant roar, launched himself full pelt at the naked girl. He came from behind his leader like a charging bull, hands outstretched to grab her by the throat. She turned slightly so as to face him and at the very last moment, with a movement that could be missed within the blink of an eye, she ducked down and as his heavy body started to fall over her she stood upright, her hands pushing upwards and with a strong expulsion of her breath he sailed over her, somersaulted and landed with a scream and a bone-jarring thump on the concrete. In the study, the Headmistress had reached for the phone. In the playground Rachel did not turn to see what had happened to her attacker but kept her eyes fixed firmly on Causten. He seemed to come out of his trance and a feral look came across his face. The possible realisation of the shattering of his ambitions at the hands of this one small girl was like a red rag to a bull, and being seized by the similar type of fury that had beset his friend, he took a flick-knife from his pocket and it flew open at his touch. At that moment two things happened.

"Coward!" shouted a voice in the crowd and this was taken up by even some of the erstwhile supporters of the gang. The chanting grew in volume with every passing moment.

"Coward! Coward! Coward! Coward!" the crowd roared. The feral look was dying in his eyes and the knife fell from his fingers. He kicked it to one side. At the same time some flashing blue lights heralded the arrival of two police cars out of which stepped heavily built police persons. An ambulance appeared a moment later, the men making straight for Jumbo's supine body and starting their investigation of his condition. Rachel broke eye contact with her opponent and walked back to where Alice was still standing motionless holding her clothes. The two girls gazed into each other's eyes and smiled slightly. Two policewomen were detailed to stand in front of the unclothed girl while she dressed herself in reverse order and the police sergeant approached the boy who had just dropped the knife.

"William Causten, I am arresting you for disturbing the peace and having in your possession a prohibited weapon with intent to wound. Anything you say will be taken down and may be used in evidence against you in a court of law. You have the right to remain silent." After picking up the discarded knife, carefully placing it in an evidence bag and writing some legend on its label, one of the officers led the now silent and badly shaken boy towards the police cars. A police van appeared on the scene. The sergeant called out the remaining three members of the gang by name and told them to get into the police van to be taken down to the station where they would be either charged or given a severe warning. Rachel had by that time exchanged happy looks with Alice and completed her dressing. She went up to the policeman and asked if she could say something to the three boys. He looked at her speculatively for a moment, then nodded his consent.

"Mickey Peters," she addressed one of the boys, "you will return the five pounds you stole from Anna MacVitie the other day as well as her purse. If you have lost or destroyed it you will replace it, is that clear?" The boy nodded reluctantly.

"Also," she added as the Headmistress came out of the door into the playground followed by her parents and Tom and Vera, "I have a list here." She took a sheet of paper from her satchel and held it high. "This contains a record of all the monies and articles taken from some of the more vulnerable and younger pupils by you and your friends in your gang. If all these articles are not restored to their rightful owners by this time on Monday evening this list will be pinned to the notice board for all the world to see. Returned articles and the names of the appropriators will be redacted when the articles have finally been returned or satisfactory reimbursement has been enacted and agreed.."

"And if anybody touches that list or defaces or destroys it in any way, they will be immediately expelled and reported to the police." Their Headmistress faced the assembled children with a stony face. "You will now go home, all of you, and understand for the last time that I will not tolerate bullying or intimidation of any sort in this school. You will learn to greet fresh year pupils with kindness and consideration and not as targets to prey upon. You are all dismissed, but I would like you, Anna, and young Timmy to come into my study now if you please." She turned to the sergeant. "Thank you very much for your help, Sergeant Wootton," she said. "I think you probably arrived just in time."

"Well, it might not have gone so well with this young lady, that's true," he agreed.

"I was thinking more that you arrived in the nick of time to save young Causten being lynched and these three lads having their heads banged together by this resourceful young person." She smiled on Rachel and Alice and they smiled modestly back at her. Sergeant Wootton looked a mite perplexed. He had heard a garbled version of the Giant Oak Battle, but the details had suffered so much from Chinese Whispers by the time the story reached his ears, he had dismissed it as silly gossip.

"You mean that that young girl could have dealt with those lads,?" he said incredulously.

"She dealt with that lump of bone-headed nonsense within a couple of seconds," she replied, nodding towards the still recumbent, but now moaning boy. She smiled at the memory. "We've got it all on film so you're welcome to have a look at it if their parents and the girls are agreeable."

"Could you have taken them on?" he asked Rachel directly.

"Oh yes." she replied diffidently. "Probably not as efficiently as Alice and I might have had some difficulty with Causten because of the knife and his unpredictability, but the other three would not have presented much of a challenge."

"I'll have to take your word for it," the policeman said. "So in the circumstances I don't think I will put either myself or my people in jeopardy by trying to arrest you for indecency, shall I."

"That's entirely up to you, Sergeant, but there was nothing indecent intended in my baring myself to my co-pupils. The object was to teach them a historical fact which was tied, emotionally perhaps, to the present situation, you see."

"And I am minded to accept your word for that as well, miss." He offered his hand to both Rachel and then to Alice, shook hands all round, then withdrew his forces in good order. The ambulance men had finally loaded the unfortunate Jumbo onto their vehicle and were just closing their doors preparatory to taking their patient to A & E in Bristol.

Amelia begged a word with them as they prepared to leave. She returned with the news that the patient showed signs of severe but not life-threatening concussion, probably some ribs broken plus a cracked vertebra or two. Now all I have to deal with is Jeremiah Roberts, Amelia thought. Humph, I wonder!

The two girls drove home with their respective parents having agreed to have some quality time each in their own homes. Sometimes circumstance dictated this arrangement, on other occasions they felt the need of their parent's undivided attention, a need quite reciprocated by their elders. Rachel sat in the back of their car in her mother's warm embrace.

"That was quite some show you both put on out there, my dear," her mother said affectionately. Rachel smiled faintly. "Do you think I should go to RADA instead of doing science?" she asked jokingly. "I might become another Hermione Gingold, all sinister twitchings and strange voices."

"Why Gingold?" her father demanded as they drove through the gates of the Old Rectory. "How about Boris Karloff or Peter Lorre?"

"Now you're just being silly, Daddy," Rachel said happily.

Alice and Vera waited until they got home to have a cuddle on the settee in the living room. Tom brought some freshly made mugs of tea in from the kitchen.

"Did you know Rachel was going to take the lead?" Tom asked.

"Well," Alice sighed. "I knew she had some notion of the way she wanted to go if the opportunity presented itself. She certainly didn't give me the slightest idea, but I was prepared for her to take lead at some point, so no surprise there." She was thoughtful for a moment. "No wonder she didn't tell anybody what she intended, though. She'd have been locked up first!" She giggled. "What a star though, eh?"

Meanwhile the Headmistress was having a few quiet words with Anna MacVitie and little Timmy in her study. "You are friendly with those two girls, aren't you?" she asked them both.

"Oh yes, miss," they chorused. "We think they're smashing," Timmy said enthusiastically. "I'd do anything for them," Anna added.

"In that case," the Head began, but Anna interrupted her in her rush to explain herself.

"Oh, we did, miss," she said. "We offered to stand with them if it came to a fight. We'd have outnumbered Will Causten and his gang ten times over, but they swore they could handle it and it was their fight and they didn't want us to make enemies of those boys. Also," she continued breathlessly, "they're so used to doing everything together that, much as we want them to, they're not really very good at joining in team sports and things like that. They won't take sides except to support people being bullied and suchlike." She ran down. Timmy was nodding away furiously, his little eyes shining. "They got my watch back from Harry Dodds, who swiped it off me just last week," he volunteered.

"I see," Amelia said slowly. "So they asked you not to interfere with whatever happened, is that right?"

"Yes, miss," Anna said. "They were adamant that they knew the odds and that, whatever it looked like, they were confident they could manage whatever was thrown at them and they thanked us for our offer, because about twenty of us including some of the older boys, were quite happy to take care of that lot, even that Jumbo who's a really hard case."

"Indeed, I think he might be so described," the Head agreed. "But Rachel Katz's actions came as a total surprise to you all, did they?"

"Oh yes, miss," both children nodded solemnly. "I've never seen a girl take her clothes off before," little Timmy said in an awestruck voice. "It was——— well, it was tremendous!"

"Yes, it was but I trust it is not going to set a precedent," the Head said severely.

"Who's a president?" Timmy asked innocently.

"It means that I don't want it to happen ever again. I do not want anybody to start taking their clothes off in public for any reason at all within the school grounds or by any pupils of the school anywhere else. I am obviously going to have to make a public announcement about that. It is perhaps fortunate, or unfortunate I'm not exactly sure which, that next week is the half-term break!" She stood up. "Now, run along both of you. I thank you for our little talk. If you can contain yourselves I would be grateful if you would not broadcast our conversation except in the most guarded tones, if that is possible."

"That means keep your lip buttoned, young Timmy," Anna said to the small boy as they left the school together. "Now, I shall see you to your home. Will your mother be worried about you, do you think?"

"I expect the Head will telephone her," he replied confidently. "She's ever so good about things like that." He took the older girl's hand as they walked down the street. "Will you marry me when I get older," he asked her wistfully.

Anna looked down at the quaint little face peering up so trustingly at her. "Well, we'll see, Timmy, we'll see." she said. "You'll have to wait a few years and I'm a lot older than you, you know."

"That's OK," he said contentedly."I can wait."

That evening Sergeant Wootton related the afternoon's events to his wife. "Extraordinary grasp of the English language that young girl has," he commented. "A walking encyclopaedia she is. Quite out of the ordinary. Don't fancy that lad's chances much, young Causten. Proper little masterpiece he is and no mistake."

"What's so good about this young miss, then?" his wife demanded tartly. "She's not English, is she? with a name like Katz, that's foreign that is. Too many foreigners over here now, if you asks me!" She sniffed. He regarded his life partner with some distaste. There were times when he found himself positively disliking her.

Jeremiah Roberts turned up at the school gates some time after Amelia Fairweather had left. Finding the gates all locked securely he let himself in the rear entrance with his own key and taking the bunch of keys from the janitor's cubby-hole prowled round the building checking all the doors. The only room which denied him access was the headmistress's study. Searching for the appropriate key he found it missing from the bunch in his hand. Puzzled, but not unduly alarmed, he replaced the bunch on their hook and let himself out of the building.

Anna, having delivered her young charge safely back to his family home, continued her own progress homewards. The picture of her recent companion's face peering up at her stayed with her and stirred up a train of thought which she began to find amusing. The idea of her nigh on six feet of solid bone and muscle wedded to the diminutive little Timmy brought to mind the comment of her laconic father on seeing a picture of a pint-sized television luminary with his tall and slender lady friend. "When yer toes to toes, yer nose is innit, when yer nose to nose, yer toes is innit." he had said to the mirth of the dinner table. Combined, the events she had just witnessed in the playground and young Timmy's devoted offer made her double up and she collapsed onto a convenient garden wall shaking with laughter. The local Church of England vicar noticing her shaking shoulders from where he had pinning a leaflet to the notice board outside his church, came solicitously over to the girl. "Are you all right, my child?" he enquired, "What has upset you so?"

"Oh dear, vicar," tears of laughter were streaming down the girl's face. "It's just that," she broke off in another fit of laughter and then repeated her father's words, while struggling to her feet and stumbling off down the road. The vicar was confused and at a loss to understand why these words should have caused such hysteria. He was a very innocent young man.

****

When Rachel had held the list up to her fellow pupils she had forgotten that the school wouldn't reconvene until the Monday week as it was the official half-term. She was. though, fully aware that the piece of paper contained no list of crimes and their perpetrators, but was merely a bluff designed to fool the guilty to reveal themselves and the victims to come forward and advance their names for repossession of their valuables. If the bluff were to work of course it would have to remain a closely guarded secret. Alice would have guessed its dubious authenticity immediately but the Head would have to be brought into the deception for it to have a good chance of success. They could at least start with the few cases of which she was sure. However, that was a problem for the next days. At the moment she was trying to get to sleep, but being so unusually on her own, she was missing the companionship and warmth she normally experienced. After a restless hour or so she got out of bed dressed in her nightshirt and tiptoed to her parent's bedroom door on which she tapped gently.

"Come in darling," her mother's quiet voice came from inside the room and Rachel opened the door to find her mother still awake and reading by the bedside light. She understandingly lifted the bedclothes for Rachel to crawl between her and her husband. "I expect you're really rather exhausted, aren't you?" she said. "Perhaps, but I'm also restless and lonely," Rachel confessed. "Do you think Alice is feeling the same?"

"I wouldn't be at all surprised, my love," Rebecca said kindly. "But she probably has the good sense to be doing exactly what you are doing, wouldn't you think?"

Rachel snuggled down into the warm space between her parents. "Do you think we'll ever grow up?" she asked wonderingly.

"Well, that's exactly what you are both doing and, come to think of it, as are we all, in one way or another." But Rachel was fast asleep.

Alice, on the other hand, had made no bones about asking her parents if she could sleep with them that night and they had made no bones about telling her that she was ruining their sex lives, conspiring to break up an admittedly already dysfunctional family by her totally immoral behaviour and that this sort of thing should have been put a stop to after the age of two. Why was she so scared of the dark? She was a big girl now and should have got over that! Alice said a rude word and Tom carried her upstairs in her pajama's and threw her onto their bed. Vera followed them into the bedroom and they tickled her until she was almost hysterical with laughter and then they settled down for a good night's sleep; Alice happily dreaming of Rachel flying over the moon dressed in a silvery frock which melted into stardust as she swooped round and landed beside her in the pastoral meadow of her phantasy, her parents sleeping peacefully with the knowledge that their daughters were indeed beyond the price of rubies.

CHAPTER XII

The next day, the Saturday preceding the mid-term break, was bright and sunny and the two girls were up betimes and had arranged to have a day cycling over the moors and seeing if they could get as far as Exmoor and visit some of the wild ponies there. However they first of all had to see to their own animals, take them for a ride, tend to their needs and muck out their stables, which meant that they might not be able to fulfil their ambitions for Exmoor that day. "Never mind," Tom said to Alice as she sat down for breakfast, "Be back by about 6.00 for an early dinner. We'll see if we can get your headmistress to come over this evening as I think we have some things to discuss about the future, don't you?"

"I jolly well do," said Alice. "There are going to be repercussions from that business yesterday, and we had better be prepared for the worst. If Causten's father gets belligerent in defence of his son or Jumbo Edwards starts proceedings for damages, we'll have to be sure of our ground. Well," she added firmly. "we've nothing to blame ourselves for, have we? ? I did extend the olive branch of peace and if they chose to spit on it that`s their bad luck."

"I know, but if the press gets hold of it, we'll get a lot of unwelcome publicity," said her father.

"Of course, Dad, and I hope we haven't got you and Rachel's parents into danger, but we can't stop them taking counsel about suing us for damages, can we?"

"No," Vera said. "But we can get the press to keep their noses out of it. I got in touch with our handlers last night and they'll make sure that it never gets as far as the nationals. I don't think either Edwards senior, or that braggart Causten, will risk having the family name dragged through the mud on account of the disgraceful behaviour of their offspring. I think any threat will come from that Roberts fellow once he discovers he's been rumbled and his plans for his elevation have been scuppered."

"Which is why we should have a chat with Amelia tonight. She's a very sensible woman, but I think she needs support, especially in the face of the underhand challenge to her authority which has been waged since she was taken ill." Tom helped himself to some toast. "All being well, I think we should all go away for a few days next week. Just up sticks and go somewhere different. How about Cornwall?"

"How about Exmoor?" Alice said. "I want to see the wild ponies and so does Rachel."

"If we start off early tomorrow, we could see them on the way down, why not," Vera suggested.

"Of course," Alice agreed. "So, what's the plan, then? We have pony time this morning and then have the rest of the day in the forest, then back to early dinner and off to the wilds of Cornwall in the morning?"

"Sounds good to me," Tom said. "I'll get Jerry to look after the shop and promise him a fortnight's paid holiday in return. He'd do it for free anyway. He loves being in the shop, especially when I'm not there to annoy him!"

Alice finished her breakfast, and asked Vera if she could make some sandwiches for their lunch. "You're not going to feast off the fruits of the forest today then?" her mother enquired innocently. "Surely there will still be a goodly selection of grubs and larvae to give you protein? Added to the variety of fungi and lichens available at this time of the year, not to mention ants' nests, and I think you would return well nourished."

"Very well, mother," said Alice. "Between us we have enough money to have lunch at the Bedford, but if we over-indulge, we will tell Jack and Betty to put it on your account, shall we?"

"Certainly you may," Vera agreed sweetly. "We will then deduct the amount from your pocket money over the forthcoming weeks or perhaps I shall telephone the Bedford Arms and instruct the owners to serve you what you want, but you will have to do the washing up in payment."

"I see that I shall have to notify my colleague about your attitude and ask her to make up our lunch-boxes. Her parents are not so criminally neglectful of their daughter's needs as are evidenced in this household. No wonder this is such a dysfunctional family!" She stuck her nose in the air and went to fetch her small backpack from the cupboard under the stairs. Tom appeared with two lunch-boxes.

"I've cut you some cheese, marmite and lettuce sandwiches and there are also apples and dates and dried figs. The water bottles are filled with tap water and you are a very naughty child so have a lovely day and try to make it back in time for supper tonight. I think that your headmistress needs you." He bent down and kissed her. Alice thanked him prettily and turned to her mother and embraced her. "Farewell, you evil woman," she said. "I hope your hair goes all straight and your toenails curl." Vera kissed her fondly. "Sweet thing!" she murmured, giving her a hug.

****

"How was your night?" asked Rachel as they saddled up their ponies. "It was lovely," Alice replied. "They let me into their bed, because I knew if I was on my own I'd have an awful time getting to sleep. I mean, why is it that we can't get to sleep on our own? Everybody else does."

"Well, I think they don't really like it, but even when you've got just a brother or sister in the same room, parents start separating their kids and our parents always let us do what we wanted. We've always slept together even when we were tots and suddenly being without anybody else is always odd. "

"Did you go in with Rebecca and Joseph last night then?" Alice asked her.

"Eventually. I lay tossing and turning and feeling a bit mis. Then I went and knocked on their door and Mum was still awake reading and she just pulled the bedclothes back and I crept in and fell fast asleep almost immediately. It was all so warm and nice. I think I'll always need someone to sleep with if I can't have you."

"Well, you're my first choice too," Alice said giggling. "They were so funny with me last night." She told her friend about the riotous bedtime the previous evening. Rachel laughed.

"They really are something else, aren't they!"

That evening they were gathered round the kitchen table, Rebecca and Joseph had turned up as well and Amelia was bringing both families up to date concerning the fate of the four boys taken away by the police and the unfortunate Jumbo Edwards who was, of course, still in hospital. Will Causten had been charged but released to the custody of his father pending a hearing at the magistrates' court first thing on Monday morning. The three other boys had been given a stern warning concerning their behaviour and told to make a list of all monies and possessions which they had purloined from their victims, with the instructions that they were to make immediate restitution of these articles on pain of prosecution for failed compliance. They were allowed until the following Monday evening, as Rachel had demanded, to satisfy the police that they had made complete restitution. They would then be under an obligation of good behaviour until such time as the police were satisfied that such good behaviour had indeed become ingrained and that they were reformed characters. They would then be deemed to be considered respectable citizens. Will Causten and Jumbo Edwards would both be charged with criminal conspiracy to inflict grievous bodily harm on two young girls who were innocent of any crime or indecent behaviour. Their parents were duly notified of the serious view the police were taking of the unjustified malice shown towards the two girls and that Sergeant Wootton, who was in charge of the case, was in no mind to treat the malefactors lightly.

However, the fact remained that the *éminence grise* behind the malice was an unsuspected factor in the mind of the good sergeant. He was puzzled by the whole affair and couldn't entirely understand how Mrs Fairweather, a likeable and competent Headmistress, had allowed this state of affairs to escalate. She had certainly warned him that very afternoon that she expected trouble at the school after the last class, and that there might be a serious situation developing, but she also said that she was not certain exactly what it was, but would he be able to come to the school at a moment's notice with reinforcements if she called him. He had promised to be in readiness and, knowing her to be a truthful and reliable person, had no doubts that what she had told him was very possible. Mulling it over that evening, he still couldn't understand how it was that these rough and somewhat loutish boys had demonstrated such hostility and rage against two perfectly pleasant and well-behaved younger girls. It was a fairly well known fact that they were devoted to each other, but that was true of some other same sex couples, and certainly was no reason for censure, remark or disapproval. The routing of the gang the previous year surely could not have still rankled with the boys as they had ignored the girls for the rest of the academic year, according to gossip. No, something or someone had been stirring the pot while the headmistress was away. At last Sergeant Wootton had found the missing element. He picked up the phone.

****

Amelia's first words after they had settled down to coffee following a very pleasant meal cooked by Vera and Tom, in tandem as it were, was to give them the news that the estimable Sergeant Wooden had applied his deductive skills to fathoming out the nigger in the woodpile, so to speak, (political correctness not having gathered any currency at that time in 1970s Britain). The difficulty would lie in laying the blame at his door and indeed, all would possibly have gone well enough for Jeremiah Roberts if he had kept his head and said nothing. Will Causten, when arrested, had maintained a surly attitude and remained sullenly mute. The stricken Jumbo was in no fit state to be questioned and the other three boys were assumed to have been under the sway of their leader and so were not questioned further at the time. It is possible that with some careful examination they might have revealed the source of his collusion in the enterprise, but by the time the sergeant had teased out the missing thread of the conspiracy, all five had been represented by a local firm of solicitors, who occasionally undertook *pro bono* work for the accused, and would probably have advised their clients to say nothing about any involvement with the Deputy Head.

Jeremiah Roberts, however, was going to save them all the bother by his subsequent actions. These commenced the following morning when he went to collect his Saturday newspapers at the newsagents in West Street. Inside the shop, Mrs Wilkins, silly old chatterbox that she was, broadcast the news to Mr Eric Todd, the newsagent, that there had been a right old kerfuffle at that school the previous afternoon. The police had been called and one of them boys, that Jumbo Edwards, had been carted off in an ambulance to Bristol Infirmary were he were a-lying at Death's Door having suffered near fatal injuries from being hurled by a naked woman over her shoulder like a sack of potatoes. And then, half a dozen or more young lads had been carted off in the police van and charged with attempted murder and the Headmistress, that Amelia Fairweather, had read the Riot Act and sent everybody home.

The Deputy Headmaster was horrified. What on earth had happened? He had expected to hear that perhaps there had been a bit of a fight at the school and two young females had been hurt and that the headmistress had not been on the premises to contain the disturbance, but this? Edwards in hospital? Some boys arrested? What was going on?

"Excuse me, I couldn't help overhearing. What on earth had been happening at my school?"

"Oh hullo, Mr. Roberts," the elderly chatterbox turned round and the newsagent also became aware of the man standing behind her. "Well, I did hear as what I've just been a-telling of to Mr Todd here, 'tho I expect he's heard it already if I knows him!" She chuckled. "He allus lets me give him the news but I knows he knows more than I does." They both laughed heartily.

"But is it true that one of the boys has been taken to hospital?"

"Thing is, Mr. Roberts sir," the newsagent leant over the counter conspiratorially to inform him, "Those young girls served them like they did last year in the woods. You'd 'ave thought they'd 'ad more sense after last time, wouldn't you. Apparently that young Jumbo Edwards charged at that Rachel Katz and she just dodged 'im somehow and over 'er shoulder 'e goes flying. Crash, thump, 'its the deck! Wallop!"

"They say she didn't have a stitch on when she did it," Mrs Wilkins contributed. "I suppose it maddened him, poor soul. He always were a bit daft, that Edwards boy, like his father really. Sandwich short of a picnic, you ask me."

He paid for his papers in a daze, but managed to leave the shop without further comment. Inside he was in a turmoil of worry. If only he could get a first hand account of what had happened. It sounded very exaggerated and he couldn't credit much of it. Why on earth would the girl have taken her clothes off? What could have possessed her to do such a thing? Surely there was some mistake here. His dilemma was compounded by not knowing whom to approach. His allies were apparently out of commission because of the proceedings of the police. No member of the staff would have been present nor was the janitor, nor even, as far as he knew, was the headmistress. No, that was wrong. What had the woman said? The Headmistress had read the Riot Act? But surely, she had not been there. He had seen her trot off homewards, so it couldn't have been her – or could it? Had she returned for something and got involved with the proceedings? But why had she not put a stop to it if she was there? Why let it go on and who had called the police? It was all very confusing.

He was by now in a state of blind panic. If he had read his Sun Tzu, or even, come to that, ever heard of the ancient classic, The Art of War, he would have known to remain quiet until such time as the other side brought the matter up and only then to proceed cautiously in an evaluation of the strength of the opposition. Being unskilled in such matters, he decided that he must, at all costs, get an authentic account of what had happened the previous evening. The likeliest source of information obviously lay with one of the schoolchildren and recalling that Saturday mornings usually witnessed some games activity on the school playing fields he made his way there in search of enlightenment.

There was indeed a football match in progress refereed by one of the junior teachers. A small crowd of onlookers were watching the match and cheering the players on with hopeful enthusiasm. The season had only recently started and these matches were played to eliminate the weaker players and pick the best for their inter-school matches which would take place later in the year. Roberts strolled along the sidelines looking for a suitable candidate for interrogation.

"Henson, isn't it?" he asked of a small boy, who had been jumping up and down with enthusiasm during a particularly daring breakthrough by one of the players towards his opponent's goal. "Timmy Henson, I believe?"

Timmy, fresh from his recent amorous venture with the delectable but unsuitable Anna, felt distinctly apprehensive confronted by the Deputy Head. So far he had managed to keep a safe distance from the teacher, of whom he was secretly terrified. The sight of this rather large man with receding black hair, small toothbrush moustache, flapping black gown and pale luminous eyes that were almost hypnotic in their stillness, chilled him thoroughly. "Yes, sir," he answered falteringly, wondering why he was being thus addressed.

"I wonder, Henson," Roberts said ingratiatingly, "whether you could afford me some information."

"I'll try, sir, if I can," Timmy said nervously, having a very good idea in which area the master wished enlightenment.

"Let us just wander away from the game for a moment, if you would be good enough," Roberts continued. "Am I correct in assuming you were present in the playground yesterday after school finished?" He observed the small boy's reluctant acknowledgement of his question. "Yes, of course you were," he confirmed. "Now, young Henson, would you please relate to me the sequence of events as they happened, starting perhaps with a breakdown of the principal characters involved." He led the boy away from the sparse line of spectators. Timmy looked back longingly at the football pitch. "I won't keep you long, Henson, so the more concise and accurate you are the sooner you will be free to return to your game. Come now, who were in the centre stage, as it were? I take it that most of the school witnessed the proceedings?"

"Oh yes, sir," Timmy confessed reluctantly. "I think pretty much we were all there, sir."

"Well?" Roberts raised his tufted eyebrows and stared luminously at the boy. (It was like being interrogated by an enormous black owl, Timmy confessed afterwards.)

"Well, sir, there was Will Causten and Jumbo Edwards and Mickey Peters and two more of Will Causten's friends but I don't know their names, please sir."

"Very well, go on, who else was there?"

"Well sir, they were in a bunch like and then Alice Darwin and Rachel Katz came out and faced them, sir and Alice said something about shaking hands and not having a fight, sir."

"Oh, they were going to have a fight, were they?"

"Oh yes, sir." Timmy was warming up to his narration. "Will Causten had challenged them to a fight, because he didn't like them, sir. I think it was because they stopped him bullying the younger girls and boys, sir and taking their money off them and they took my watch from me and they are bullies sir."

"Go on, Henson," Roberts said icily. "Tell me what happened when Darwin offered her hand in submission."

"Oh, I don't think it was submission, it was just an offer to drop the challenge, sir. Neither of them were submissive, sir." As Timmy became more wrapped up in the retelling of the conflict, the Deputy Head became more agitated. "Then Rachel said something to Alice which I didn't hear and then told Will Causten that he and his gang were bullies and that she would even out any advantage he thought she had and then she took all her clothes off sir, and told us all about how her family had fled from the Nazis and how the Nazis had melted all the Jews down for soap, sir, and it was all very sad and quite a few of the girls were crying and it made me feel very sad but I didn't cry - well, not at the time, anyway," he added truthfully.

"So tell me, Henson, what happened next? Did she attack Causten?"

"Oh no, sir, that was Jumbo, sir" Timmy protested.

"Do you mean to tell me that Edwards attacked Causten?" Jeremiah Roberts was barely managing to control his fury.

"Oh no sir," Timmy said cheerfully. "He went straight for Rachel, sir. He charged her like a wild bull, sir."

"And what was her response? You tell me she was standing there facing him with no clothes on?"

"Yes sir, but I've never seen anything like it. She sort of ducked and then bobbed up again and Jumbo went sailing over her head and landed upside down on the concrete, sir. I thought he was dead, sir, but he started moaning a bit later when the ambulance men came."

"Yes, yes, but what happened next?" Timmy looked a bit puzzled, then his face cleared.

"Oh yes sir. Sorry sir, I got a bit lost there. Well, then Will Causten took out a flick-knife and looked as if he was going to attack Rachel, but she didn't move a muscle, sir, just stood there waiting for him to make a move and then somebody shouted 'Coward!' and then some of the other kids took it up and everybody was catcalling him, sir and then the police arrived and arrested the boys and Rachel put her clothes back on and then we all went home, sir."

"I see," his interlocutor said frigidly, staring into the middle distance with an unfathomable expression on his saturnine countenance. "Well, thank you, Henson, you may now return to your game." With which he turned abruptly away and made his way homeward. How long he sat in his small sitting-room in his little house on the edge of he village is not recorded. However, from the evidence of his housekeeper he must have smoked his way through a number of packets of Capstan Full Strength cigarettes and drunk the contents of two bottles of single malt whisky with beer chasers over the course of the weekend. His consumption of solid food was limited to a large packet of extra strong cheddar to the accompaniment of an even larger tin of assorted biscuits which he had bought the previous week in anticipation of the small celebratory party he had intended holding on his installation as Headmaster. Pride goeth before destruction and a haughty spirit before a fall, as Proverbs has it. Certainly that was the thought which crossed Amelia Fairweather's mind when she heard the news.

Later that Saturday morning, when the football match had ended, Timmy Henson made his way to Amelia's house and asked her husband, who had answered the door, whether he could to speak to the Headmistress. He invited the little boy in and asked him whether he would like a glass of homemade lemonade and a biscuit while he waited for the return of the lady in question as she had just popped out to get some more milk. Timmy accepted the offer as his throat was quite dry from having cheered on his friends at the match. Henry had no sooner settled his visitor into an armchair and supplied the required items than the front door was opened and then Amelia Fairweather was sitting opposite Timmy and listening to the report of his interrogation by her deputy.

"Did he not ask you who else was there at the confrontation?" she asked him wonderingly.

"No, miss, he seemed to lose interest when I said that we all went home after Rachel put her clothes on again." Timmy had obviously been impressed and fascinated by Rachel's disrobing and subsequent re-robing. Amelia hoped that this image, which was patently fixed firmly in the child's mind, would have a benign effect on his later relationship with the opposite sex. She of course had no idea that it had already produced the precocious result of turning his mind to future matrimony, but would probably have applauded his courage in making the heartfelt proposal to his giant friend.

"Well, thank you, Timmy, for coming and telling me about that. I think it would be better if we kept that just between us for a few days if you don't mind." Timmy, thus appealed to, felt quite proud of himself and promised that his lips were sealed until such time as his Headmistress lifted the embargo.

"So tell me, Timmy, did Anna MacVitie see you home safely yesterday?"

"Oh yes miss, thank you." A smile came over his face. "She's a super girl, isn't she, miss," he said enthusiastically. "Indeed, I think she certainly is pretty super, Timmy," the Headmistress agreed.

"I asked her to marry me," the little boy continued happily. "She said she would think about it but that she was a bit older than me, so we will have to wait quite a while, won't we?"

"You will, Timmy, you will." Strangely, she took the boy's remark in the spirit it was meant. She knew people like this, who appeared simple and unpretentious but had the knack of keeping their goals in view without wavering or giving up on them even if the outcome seemed to be impossible of achievement to an onlooker. Consequently the result was that their pronouncements became reality more often in the course of time than the reverse. She studied the little chap seated opposite her who was contentedly sipping at his lemonade and getting through a large plate of biscuits at an astonishing rate. His was a nature not uncommon in rural England and indeed in many other parts of the world, which has a mixture of sanguinity and common sense, level headedness with a steadfast passion that is quietly creative and life affirming. She could well believe that Timmy's devotion would remain constant and that in the due passage of time, Anna MacVitie might well become Mrs. Timmy Henson, still five years older than her husband, but settled as her mate for life who would grow closer to her younger husband as the years passed. There was something almost Dickensian in the child and she realised afresh how much she liked children and wanted to give them all a good education which would enable them to lead fruitful and benign lives amongst their fellow beings. She felt badly about Will Causten and Jumbo Edwards and earnestly wished she could have done more to lead them into a healthier outlook. At the same time she knew full well that the odds were seriously stacked against her. The Causten family and also the Edwards to a certain extent, belonged to a bible thumping group which met at a onetime Quaker Meeting House. They called themselves the Eleventh Hour Immersionists or some such nonsensical title, she recalled, but with none of the wit of Mr. Noel Coward. In reality it was a form of mean spirited, misogynistic, intolerant fundamentalism that incited hatred of anyone or anything free of the herd mentality or displaying evidence of originality of thought; it encouraged an abhorrence of affection, charity or even hope. She wondered whether Jeremiah Roberts was also an adherent of the faith. All this she faithfully related to her friends at the Darwin household that evening.

    The following day, however brought news of a new development. The Darwins with the two young girls had driven down to Cornwall first thing in the morning, leaving the animals in charge of the Katz household, as they were unable to arrange for locums at such short notice. The fresh development was the unusual appearance of the Deputy Headmaster appearing in the saloon bar of the Bedford Arms that evening. To Jack Hamilton's experienced eye, the teacher was in that state of semi-paralytic alcoholism which principally affected solitary whisky drinkers. Their motor functions had the appearance of normality but to the experienced eye it was obvious that the man was in a dangerous state which could tip either which way. He could possibly get through an evening being topped up by a small but regular intake of his particular tipple and make his way home without mishap. On the other hand the slightest upset to his mental equilibrium could result in either a ludicrous display of hostility leading to an ineffectual pugnacity, or a complete physical collapse and unconsciousness. With a man of Robert's frustrated rage, there was no knowing which way it would go. Although he rarely came into contact with him, Jack knew that he was not the sort of character that was accepted as a 'gentleman drunk'. He was also perturbed, therefore, when he realised that after ordering a large Famous Grouse, Roberts made his way over to where Edwards senior was holding court and relating to anybody who could be bothered to listen how his son had been viciously attacked and virtually paralysed by the devious and underhand methods of that pair of young harpies who should have been expelled from that school a year ago and were no better than wild animals and everybody knew what to do with wild animals that attacked innocent people.

The regulars ignored him and let him rant away. Jack had abandoned any idea of barring him as it would have only made things worse. He allowed him beer but no spirits and enjoined upon him to keep his complaint at a reasonable level and his temper strictly in check.

Roberts asked him how his son was doing, then receiving an invitation from the father of the injured boy, he sat down at his table. The two men eyed each other cautiously. The conversation superficially touched on Jumbo's condition. He had recovered consciousness whilst in the ambulance, and on admission to the A&E department of the Bristol Royal Infirmary, it was discovered that there was a hairline fracture of the sacrum and some concussion. He had been badly shaken up, but would be home within a few days unless the doctors found any reason to keep him under observation. He had little memory of the incident, but according to his father, had become incensed by the Katz girl's blatant disregard of decency. Edwards senior discoursed for some time on the subject of the outrageous behaviour of the two girls who flaunted all decency and modesty with their infamous antics. Jeremiah's eyes began to glaze over as the tirade swept over him and the whisky's effect began to wane. At last he could stand it no longer. He stood up, went to the bar and came back bearing refills. He also carried an extra triple scotch which was solely for his own use. Edwards looked at it speculatively.

"I have been given strict instructions that this is not for you," Roberts informed him. "Apparently you are not to be trusted with hard liquor." Edwards glared.

"Bloody cheek," he muttered. "Suppose I'd better be careful, though." The two men eyed each other suspiciously, wondering who was going to moot the subject dearest to their hearts. At heart they were both thugs, of course. Edwards was a blustering bullying type, the sort of heavy duty bruiser who collects bad debts for gangsters. Roberts was a manipulating, controlling type who is happy for others to do his heavy work for him. Their antipathy towards both girls was not fed from the same source though. Edwards feared and consequently despised anybody who was too well liked or who stuck out from the general run of ordinary citizens. Roberts hated the girls also on account of their courageous individuality and strength of mind, but also because he regarded them as a stumbling block to his ambitions and their partisanship with the Headmistress. The two men also harboured more atavistic and deeply held secret lusts and fears of women in general and the advance of the female in contemporary life. It was perhaps unfortunate that both girls had not the slightest inkling that they themselves were in any way unusual. Both their parents had of course cultivated a cloak of semi-invisibility round themselves for very sensible professional reasons. They were accepted as functionaries in their public capacities, but nobody really knew much about any of them and nobody thought to enquire any further. They were very private people. Their children were also reclusive but attracted much more attention because of their activities and also because of their personalities. They were always polite and well-mannered, but went their own way. When challenged they either defused the situation or knocked it on the head as has been recounted.

For those who have a belief that there is no such thing as coincidence and that everything is interconnected with the unfolding of the universe, I shall now give a hint of things to come. As the malevolence and malignity of the two men fed off each other, a circumstance was unfolding in a neighbouring town which was leading to a happenstance of some consequence concerning the welfare of Alice, Rachel and also the innocent little Timmy. The lives of all three of them were soon to be placed in horrifying jeopardy, which may go some way to supporting the hypothesis that what doesn't kill you, strengthens you - well, sometimes, anyway!

So I think we will leave our two villains in the pub poisoning not only their own minds but the air around them and pouring vitriol into the ether where it would eventually settle in the hearts and minds of a pair of truly vile men and their horrendous female protector. But enough of these horrors for the moment; let us return to more agreeable matters.

CHAPTER XIII

While the Darwins senior and their two young girls were on pleasure bent in the wilds of Cornwall, Amelia Fairweather had been gathering information concerning the activities of her *bête noir* and was strangely distressed by an account of his Sunday visit to the Bedford Arms. This had been related to her by Jack Hamilton who would never, in the normal course of events, have dreamt of tittle-tattling about his customers, but felt bound on this occasion to warn the good lady of the threat he had overheard Roberts make to Edwards concerning herself. The thought crossed her mind that if Roberts was having recourse to stimulants in order to keep his spirits up after the failure of his move to unseat her, then he must be in quite a parlous state. Of Edwards she had no mind nor any concern. Her Deputy, on the other hand, was a good teacher, an intelligent and well read man who was in the process of throwing it all away on a hopeless cause. That she was an integral part of this vain pursuit she was only too aware. Consequently she felt duty bound to put the man back on his feet and functioning properly again. Revenge was now not an option as far as she was concerned, but alongside a desire to reinstate him as a respected pedagogue and useful member of society, was an equally powerful determination to protect her two young protégés from further mischief at his hand. The question remained as to how this was to be achieved. To march up to his house, demand entrance and read him the Riot Act was an attractive idea but with little likelihood of success. He might, of course, capitulate and follow whatever advice she had to give him with a good heart and the will to redeem himself, but that, she realised, would most probably be a non-starter. She had an alarming vision of the door being slammed firmly in her face and his return to even more self-medication with the most harmful results. She needed good counsel. It was mid-Monday morning. Henry was at his bank and she would not, in all fairness, have wished to disturb him with her worries. She rang the Katz household.

Joseph was still home although Rebecca was at the surgery. They staggered the hours whenever possible which made home-life a bit easier with the dogs and the girls when the Darwins were absent. Joseph suggested that she have an off-the-record word with Sergeant Wootton as he, Joseph, could not put himself forward as a medical consultant, being an interested party in the situation, but was of the opinion that Roberts needed medical help on a number of fronts and that perhaps a police psychiatrist or physician might be available and could approach the man on neutral territory as it were. Amelia went to see the Sergeant at the police station.

"This is not," she said firmly, "a complaint of any sort and I hope that what I have to say will be treated in complete confidence."

"That's perfectly understood, Mrs. Fairweather," he replied equably. "I won't take any official action if there is any other way of dealing with this affair. I take it that, apart from the safety and further peaceful running of your school, you are concerned about the behaviour of a certain gentleman who has been giving you cause for some alarm very recently."

"Tactful as ever, Sergeant Wootton," she replied. "I think it must be obvious that Mr. Roberts is in a very bad and unhappy place at the moment and is coping with it as best he can by injudicious applications to the whisky bottle and morose and unseemly discussions with a certain relative of one of the chief culprits from last Friday evening's disgraceful attack on the two children. The brandishing of a flick-knife naturally raises the reprehensibility of the boy who produced it, and I think the sternest retribution must be meted out to him on that count alone. I am concerned, though, apart from the welfare of the two girls, that my Deputy should be treated as a troubled soul and not an out and out villain. He has much to offer the school but he is obviously in the grip of some mental breakdown. He needs medical and probably psychological attention and I hope you are not contemplating incarcerating him or charging him with any crime," she finished.

"You do realise, Headmistress," the Sergeant said grimly, "that he was, in fact, the mastermind, if I may so put it, behind the whole event. I don't think those boys would have got so exercised in their minds about having some sort of showdown with the girls if Roberts had not chivvied them on and heaped coals upon the fire of their still smouldering resentment. What's more, you yourself could have put a stop to it by challenging Roberts and those two young ruffians with instant dismissal if they had carried out such an attack."

"I realise it only too well, Sergeant," she said sadly. "We all knew it was coming and I went round to the girls' families and we discussed it at length. The outcome was that they thought they could handle it well enough on their own, but if I did exactly what you have just suggested, the plotters would have totally denied any conspiracy of intention, but perhaps successfully ambushed them at a later date when they were least expecting it. I could hardly dismiss Mr. Roberts with such a tenuous accusation. He would have turned the tables on me nicely, I think."

"Well, in that case I agree with you that it was wise to let them go ahead with it and catch them in the act. We have been known to countenance such a procedure with good results but you were taking something of a risk, surely, with the safety of those girls."

"Well, do you know, Sergeant, I can honestly say that I think if they had been in any real danger, their supporters would have dealt with that gang very effectively. Anna MacVitie for one, is a friend of Alice and Rachel and she is a big tough girl who would have no qualms about coming to their rescue – and she's not the only one. Many of the boys had also pledged their support, but the two didn't want to involve others in what was their fight as they saw it. Also, of course, nobody had the slightest suspicion that Causten even possessed such a weapon. Whoever it was who started shouting 'Coward!' at them made him drop his knife. You must remember that Rachel Katz's startling nudist act had already defeated them morally, even before the Edwards boy lost his head. He really is a very silly young man – they all are, of course."

"Agreed, madam, agreed. At the same time, my position as an upholder of law and order demands that I take some action concerning your Assistant Headmaster. Now what would you have me do about him? He cannot be ignored. For one thing I imagine it will be fairly obvious that he had been condoning these boys' proposed actions and had actively encouraged them to these extremes. Added to that, his behaviour over the weekend is as blatant an admission of his complicity as could be demonstrated, in particular his cozying up to Edwards in the Bedford Arms."

Amelia sat thinking for a few moments. "I would certainly not wish to interfere or try to persuade you against your better judgement or challenge your integrity as a policeman, Sergeant

Wootton. Please believe me when I say I have every confidence in your ability to come to the right decision over any action that needs to be taken. However, he is obviously a severely sick man and a court action with the possibility of a prison sentence would, I am convinced, utterly destroy him. It would be kinder to have him hanged than for him to face such degradation."

A silence fell between them. The policeman pressed a bell on his desk and the door opened and a WPC put her head in.

"Do you think you could rustle up some tea and biscuits for us, Wendy?" he said.

"Certainly sir," she said cheerfully, and withdrew on her errand. The two of them sat in a quite companionable silence while they waited for the tea.

"I take it you have some sympathy for the man?" he asked ruminatively when the tea and biscuits finally arrived.

"I would be sorry to see any person in such confusion and pain," she replied. "Furthermore, I hate to see the waste of a good teacher and useful member of society. I don't know what has been the underlying cause of Mr. Robert's deranged behaviour, nor his extravagant hostility towards myself and those nice children, but I have always known him for a lonely man, too much wrapped up in the responsibilities of the school and with no domestic outlet for his natural needs which most of us take for granted. He is also at the age when he would begin to take stock of his life and find himself in a position inferior to that which he would have expected to be in with his qualifications and experience. To be beaten to the post by a woman must have made the disappointment even harsher to bear, and he has reverted to the sort of lonely phantasising which creates a distorted reality and the consequent undisciplined and dysfunctional behaviour. This is bad enough in a very young person, but in a man of mature years it is grotesque, dangerous and pitiful, which is why I would have him treated with compassion and not branded as a monster."

The policeman looked at the headmistress with considerable respect. "That was very well said, Mrs. Fairweather," he said, pouring them another cup of tea and passing the plate of biscuits to his visitor. She was impressed by such niceties as bone china teacups and a hot water jug to accompany the teapot, snug in it's knitted cosy.

"How do you suggest we go about it?"

"Do you have a physician on your staff, by any chance?" she asked him.

"We have more than that, we have Dr. Meadows who is the coroner and M.E. for the district. He is, as you may know, very skilled in his work and I can co-opt him for an interview with the gentleman when we pay him a visit."

"Excellent," she applauded. "If you can either ask him to visit you here, or if he would prefer, you could go to his home - I think he would probably prefer to come here, as I understand his house is a bit of a shambles at the moment - well, that's according to Margaret Heyhoe, who does for him three times a week. She said that there were empty bottles all over the place and a terrible thick fug of cigarette smoke, but she is given to exaggeration. I doubt whether he would have let himself go to that extent. He would also pull himself together after that extraordinary visit to the Bedford Arms on Sunday."

"Quite so, but what approach would you recommend? My natural feeling is to go round to his house now and throw him in our holding cell, but you have persuaded me that no real good would come of such a course of action."

"Sergeant, you have a very good reputation as a calm, sensible man who is compassionate yet upright and honest in your dealings with the inhabitants of this community, so might I suggest you use the carrot and stick approach to my colleague. I imagine he is by now riddled with guilt and remorse but has no idea how to resolve his dilemma. I think if you put the matter plainly to him that he is in peril of being arraigned for some very serious offences, but if he will come clean and confess his involvement with these lads' disgraceful behaviour, you will take no action against him on condition that he submit himself to an evaluation of his mental and physical state and willingly put himself into the hands of the professionals who can help him recover his equilibrium and sanity. I am sure you will be able to achieve this with tact and understanding and I know Dr. Meadows for a good and fair-minded man."

He thought about this for a moment. "I think that might work," he said slowly, "but if he starts any trouble with any of us, he will not be treated so kindly."

"I think, you know," Amelia said, "that he must be at the end of his tether and if it is put to him as a lifeline he will accept it gladly. As far as the school is concerned, I shall inform the staff and pupils that he has had a breakdown from overwork and unexpected responsibilities which had put too much of a strain on a far from well constitution. As this is basically the reality of the situation I can say that in all truthfulness. If he had been in his right mind he would never have hatched up such a piece of Machiavellian mischief. I will also say that it is to be hoped that he will recover and soon be back in his position as my right-hand man. It is always sensible to have one's opponents within one's sphere of influence, don't you agree, Mr. Wootton?"

"How right you are, Mrs. Fairweather," said the policeman shaking her hand at the door of his office. "But always be on your guard for the smiler with the knife and never turn your back on a rattlesnake."

"Two pieces of excellent advice, Sergeant for which I thank you, but let us pray that Mr. Roberts will be well and truly healed when - and if, of course - he returns to my school."

Amelia and the complaisant policeman parted from each other with mutual feelings of satisfaction and co-operation, she to her home to prepare some food against her husband's return at the end of a hard day at his bank, and he to telephone to Jeremiah Roberts, who agreed to come in and have a friendly chat about the occurrences at the school the previous Friday. Stanley Wootton had been in touch with Dr. Meadows who had agreed to be present at the meeting with Roberts. The Sergeant was aware that Roberts would probably know who Meadows was, but he intended merely to introduce him as a colleague without specifying his credentials. He considered that Roberts was in a muddled enough state not to understand the significance of the attendance of the medical man, so would be less alarmed at the possible outcome of the meeting. It would probably not have mattered much either way as it turned out, since the unfortunate man was in such a weakened state of self-mortification and guilt at his actions that the gentle handling of the interview by the wily Sergeant broke any defenses that he might have erected between himself and his interlocutors, to the effect that only a quarter of hour of gentle probing had unleashed a torrent of confession and lachrymosity which left the officials in no doubt that the unfortunate pedagogue was in need of help and not punishment.

They fed him tea and sympathy and Dr. Meadows arranged for a hospital car to take the miserable and shaken teacher straight to a nursing home that specialised in mentally disturbed people who were no physical danger to themselves or others. Both men had considered this was the correct course to take and were proved right in their assessment. The medical and nursing staff at the nursing home were unanimous in their good opinion of their new patient who blossomed after the preliminary shock of finding himself in strange surroundings whilst metabolising the large amounts of alcohol which were sloshing around in his system. He seemed to have accepted his fate completely and become relaxed and on the whole quite cheerful. The doctors put this down to a certain childishness in his character which had been suppressed for many years and was now, owing to the cessation of any need for controlling either himself or others, was happily finding expression in an innocence which had been thwarted for over forty years.

"He's living the life he should have lived when he was a child," one of the doctors confided to Doctor Meadows when the latter, at the bequest of the sergeant, had asked for news of their patient's progress. "Underneath the martinet was a love-starved child who needed expression. He's very fortunate. Very few people in his condition have the blessing of this sort of abreaction, mainly because they have got themselves into trouble with the law and have been branded with harsh penalties which have hardened them even further until they become adamantine criminals and almost beyond recovery. He'll grow again quite quickly when this period is over and he starts being an adult again. It may very well be that his whole personality will have changed - for the better, I should add."

Naturally Amelia and the Sergeant were delighted with the news which Dr. Meadows broke in confidence to them. But this was some weeks after the patient had been accepted into the nursing home. Amelia, on the advice of the doctors, didn't visit Roberts at any time while he was under treatment. There would have been little point anyway: she did not wish it and the nursing home was of the opinion that it might, indeed, set his recovery back if the reality of his recent behaviour was brought to the forefront of his mind too soon. In his own good time and when he was strong enough he would no doubt recall that behaviour and find the courage and strength to bring it out into the open and discuss with others what, if any, reparation could be made.

These events were still to take place, so let us return to the week of the half-term break that saw Jeremiah Roberts allow himself to be given over to the care of the nursing home, the incarceration of Will Causten in a young offenders' institute to be followed by his lieutenant on his release from hospital later that week, and the formal warning to the other three members of the gang which has already been recorded. The Headmistress was happy with the result and was preparing herself for the forthcoming Monday when she would have to make an announcement of some gravity at school assembly. She also had to find a supply teacher (or teachers) to fill the gap left by her erstwhile second-in-command and find a successor to him if only on an *ad hoc* basis. It occurred to her that it might be an opportunity to test the potential of the more experienced and able of her present staff for that position in the event that Roberts was unable to eventually return to his formal position.

The Darwins meanwhile were leaving for a jolly if somewhat rain-swept holiday in Falmouth, the heatwave of the former two months of 1976 having dried out the land and the people to the extent of aridity. This had given place to a monotonous downpour of the sort to dampen the most optimistic holiday spirits. The Darwins, being the people they were, made no complaint, but enjoyed their slow progress over the country roads, making their promised diversion to Exmoor *en route* so that the two girls could visit the wild ponies. In this they were disappointed for Exmoor was draped in a cloud of drizzle and the animals were nowhere to be seen.

"We'll come back this way," Tom promised them, "but I've a notion we're in for some settled dampness."

"Monsoon time, then. Are we going to be stuck in the hotel all day?" Alice asked. "Because we haven't brought that many books or games with us, have we!" she grumbled.

"You are of course, perfectly correct, my treasure," Vera replied patiently. "But what would ever prevent you from going out in any sort of weather short of a blizzard? A few drops of rain? Surely not!"

"Also," Tom added. "Falmouth is a very nice town and most likely has a bookshop or two from which you may purchase items of interest up to your allowance and whatever monies you have with you at the moment. They also have a public library, I believe, so that you can get the latest Barbara Cartland in most probability."

"Thank you, Papa. I'm sure we will find plenty to amuse us even if we are housebound, but exploring a strange town in the murk and fog is a delight at any time."

"Aren't we going to have fun!" Vera said happily. She turned round in her seat to face the two girls in the back of the car. "You could also consider, if you were really bored, ways in which to undermine the smooth running of the hotel in such a manner that you are not identified as the culprits but cause as much mayhem and havoc amongst those innocent pleasure-seekers as you do in your daily lives at home."

"Thank you, Mama," Alice said gravely. "We'll keep that in mind as a last resort. We really don't want to have to be asked to leave the hotel in disgrace, do we?"

"That is a consideration, to be sure, but as long as you don't feel empowered to disrobe in front of the other guests," she said looking pointedly at Rachel, "then I think that outcome will not materialise."

"What a shame, Mama," said that young person blithely. "I was sooooo looking forward to descending the ornate stairs of the hotel dressed only in my long mink coat, and just as I was about to sink into my chair at the breakfast table I, the cynosure of all eyes, would murmur, quite audibly to my adoring fans, that it was rather hot in here wasn't it, and with that I would divest myself of my magnificent fur and collapse onto my breakfast chair totally naked, signaling at the same time to the waiter to pour my coffee for me. I would then take out my very long cigarette holder and various young men in states of sexual excitement would hasten to my table with the lighters flickering in the draught from the exhaled breath of a thousand witnesses and proffer their flames to my Black Russian Sobranie."

"Which was held in the cigarette holder which was held by your blood red lips," Alice added breathlessly. "Cut and print! Bravo, Miss Katz! This will make cinematographic history. Forget Jane Fonda, forget Lauren Bacall, forget Monroe, forget Gish, Pickford and Mary Bow, forget them all. Here is, in the flesh, and boy, what flesh, the one, the only, Rachel Katz, star of stage, screen, radio and Joe's takeaway fish and chip shop of a Friday evening."

"That's me all right," Rachel agreed smugly, "You're right on the ball, kiddo."

Tom drew into the courtyard of a transport café. He turned to his wife.

"Shall we," he suggested, "just leave them here."

"Good thinking," she replied. "We'll feed them first then turn them loose. They can then either walk or hitch back home or make their own way to Falmouth."

"You'll probably get a lift in a lorry from here," Tom said kindly to the two girls who were by now hanging on, one to each arm, and jumping up and down wailing and crying like demented five-year olds. A waitress standing idly by the window watched their approach in some alarm.

"But soft!" Tom said quietly to them as they neared the entrance. "We are observed."

Immediately the two girls dropped their act and taking their parents' arms they walked demurely into the café.

"We should like," Vera said to the waitress," a pot of tea for four and baked potatoes all round with various fillings. We intend to abandon these children here after they have been fed, as they are a trial and a tribulation to all who encounter them and frankly, twelve years has been more than enough for us. You look like a kindly person," she said pleasantly to the young waitress. "They're really fairly self-sufficient and would be quite content with a single room and all found. You could put them to work with you here or rent them out for menial tasks. We would of course reimburse you for their board and lodging and a small honorarium from time to time to sweeten the deal. How does that sound?"

"Absolutely spot on," replied the damsel without so much as the bat of an eye-lid. "I'll take your orders first and then, if you can give me a month`s rent in advance, I've got a very nice little box-room in my cottage where they would be most welcome until I can get them settled with a colleague of mine who runs a very respectable little business in Cairo. You won't have any more trouble with them, I can promise you, but of course there's always the possibility that he might sell them on if they prove sub-standard!" She withdrew with a bright smile to fulfil their order and was back in a trice with a large pot of tea plus accessories.

"Just had a chat with my friend and he's delighted so they might even get shipped off tonight if that's OK with you.."

"Oh Papa, what fun," Alice clapped her little hands together in glee. "We're going off to be white slaves, Rachel, isn't that just the bee's knees?"

"Super," she crowed. "What an adventure!"

Some moments later their waitress brought their food for them. "Where are you off to?" she asked. "Or did you hope to see the ponies in the wild today?"

"Is that the only reason people visit Exmoor?" Tom asked. "To see the ponies? No, we just stopped on our way down to Falmouth."

"A bit out of your way, aren't you?" The girl lingered. "But I imagine these two young ladies are possibly rather keen to see them. Well, there's always the pony club but it's not the same as seeing them on the moors is it?" The girls smiled at her.

"I don't know really," Alice said. "We've got a couple of ponies ourselves, but I don't know if they're Exmoor or what breed they are, but we love them just the same."

"You'll miss them in Cairo, then," the waitress said mischievously.

"Oh, that's all right," Rachel said airily "We'll get a pair of young camels with our ill-gotten gains and teach them to race and play games with us." She smiled at them.

"You know, my Mum and Dad run a B&B just down the road. It's not far from the pony club, and you might like to visit us on the way back. Two double rooms free at the moment and not very expensive." She mentioned a very modest sum. "Breakfast included and you could always come in here for a meal later. but Mum never minds cooking of an evening provided as she's given enough notice. I'll leave you to your meal," she said cheerfully. "Enjoy!"

When they had finished their meal Tom waved the waitress over and paid the bill.

"Where is your parents' B&B?" he asked her.

"Just down the road. Continue as you were going, take the first turning on the left where there's a broken off signpost and it's fifty or so yards down that road on your right. There's a modest sign outside saying Bluebell Cottage, B&B, Vacancies. The vacancies sign was up when I left this morning anyway." She chuckled. "I don't think anybody would have found it in this drizzle, do you?"

"Hasn't it been open long then?" Rachel asked.

"Just this summer, so it'll take a little while for word to get around," she replied. "My Mum's name is Rita Longford and I'm Lisa. My Dad's name is Bert but he'll be out in the fields finding damp sheep all over the place. It's still a working farm but they hope to downsize in the next few years and have a change of income."

"Rushing up and down stairs in the dry instead of rushing about outside in the damp," Vera said. "Who can blame them?"

They said goodbye to the friendly waitress and called at the farmhouse. Rita Longford turned out to be a plump, jolly woman who had the good looks of her daughter but spread over a wider area. After a quick glance at the bedrooms, a large and comfortable bed in each and a cursory look around the rest of the premises, Tom made a booking for that Saturday night on their return journey and promised to ring Rita and let her know what time they expected to arrive. They then set off for Cornwall.

"That is one nice family," Vera said as they drove off.

CHAPTER XIV

Falmouth turned out to be fairly consistently damp that week, but they all had some fun exploring the lovely old town. There was a wonderful pub with armchairs and a whole library to choose from which pleased Tom and Vera who liked nothing more than a pint or two of real ale and a thriller to read. The girls opted for more energetic exploration and amused themselves by going down to the harbour in the hope of seeing one of the Tall Ships which occasionally visited the town. The biennial Tall Ships Race had in fact taken place that year but had set off from Plymouth some months earlier.

"I would really love to see one of those ships," Rachel said. "They look so beautiful and some of them have all girl crews as well. They are for young people after all."

"Yes well, you have to be between the ages of 16 and 25, I think, so we have a little while to wait, by which time I expect we will have grown out of the desire."

"I sincerely hope so," Rachel said. "It's not really our scene, is it? Though it's quite nice to dream about it sometimes and they are such lovely things."

"Yes. A spaceship now! – how about that?"

"Will you be Flesh Gordon, or shall I?"

"Take it in turns like we always do." They both giggled naughtily and returned to the hotel for lunch. The hotel itself was quite comfortable and the food simple but good. Some of the other residents were also simple but not always that good. There was the inevitable Life and Soul of the Party who, although having been frozen out of any hope of participation with his plans for jolly games which included the Darwin party, nevertheless continued his attempt to badger them into his idea of communal jollification.

"There's one in every holiday hotel usually," a retired colonel confided to Tom and Vera over a nightcap at the bar, the girls having gone to bed long since. "Poor things; think they've got to organise everybody all the time. Some of them have actually been in the war, but mostly they wish they had been for some unfathomable reason. Can't say it was the life I would have chosen voluntarily, but family, you know and convenient war. Hateful business."

"What do you do now?" Vera asked him.

"So, you spotted I wasn't retired, eh?" he laughed. "You're dead right. I might be in my sixties now, but after I left the army, I went back to school and became an entomologist, or more truthfully, I took a degree in entomology and then opened a market garden in Dorset."

"Really?" Tom said. "Whereabouts in Dorset may I ask? We often visit there on the look-out for bits and pieces for our little garden."

"Wimborne way, you know. Just outside the town. Give you an address if you'd like."

"That would be good," Tom said. "Not that we often get that far east, but you never can tell, can you?" The colonel fished a card out of his pocket and handed it to him. Tom glanced at it and said casually,

"It's strange, but petunias aren't in season at the moment, are they?"

"Just as well," the colonel replied urbanely. "They're the very devil to get rid of."

"More's the pity," Vera interposed. "My favourites are hollyhocks,"

"But who needs those nowadays!" the colonel finished off amusedly.

"Honestly, what will they think of next," Vera said wonderingly. "Just imagine having that conversation in front of a bunch of horticulturalists!"

"So what's happening?" Tom asked bluntly.

"Nothing, we hope, to worry about, but when Vera phoned us on Friday evening concerning the press, we thought we should just check on you all. You know we're keeping an eye on those two young girls of yours and are mightily impressed with them. About the coolest thing since Mata Hari is the general buzz, and if they develop as we think they might, there is the possibility of offering them some further education not universally available. It entirely depends on them and you, of course. Absolutely no pressure you can rely on that."

Tom eyed him coldly as did Vera. "Oh, there'll be pressure all right," Tom said grimly. "There always is, but we will balance that out for our children you may be sure. I expect they will take to the trade like ducks to water, but there's no guarantee at this stage."

"I know, old boy," the man said calmly. "One of the reasons I'm telling you is so that you know the support will always be there, and even more secure because of the value to us of their possible involvement at a later stage. Our assessment, which you have to admit is usually pretty accurate and fair, is that those two would make a formidable team one day. They're extremely tough for 12-year-old schoolchildren. They've got nerve and courage and skills that few people have who haven't been reared in a martial arts school. They are also highly intelligent and decent people in their own right. Of course there is a possibility that puberty will throw them haywire, but they have the strong support of two families of excellent quality and probity and I can't say fairer then that, can I? In the meantime, they have a protective eye covering their backs as much as it is possible with a self-willed couple such as those two." He finished his drink.

They shook hands with him and mentioned that they would be staying in Exmoor on Saturday night. Tom gave him the address of the B&B and they wished him goodnight.

"I rather like him," Vera said on their way upstairs. "Slippery as mercury but strangely warm-hearted."

"Quite a few of them are, surprisingly enough," Tom responded, "though you might not think so after reading le Carré and Deighton."

"Well, he's old school, really isn't he," said Vera. "Richard Hannay and that lawyer fellow who figures in those Buchan novels.".

****

The days passed quite amiably for the family and the girls scored a hit with an extremely inquisitive elderly couple who started cross-questioning them about their relationship with each other and Rachel's relationship to Tom & Vera. It was Alice who nipped it firmly in the bud.

"Rachel is my friend," she said politely. "If you wish to know anything further concerning our private lives or relationship you may apply to our solicitors. They are Fitch & Abercrombie, Lincoln's Inn Fields London E1, but I have to advise you that they are tremendously expensive, especially in the case of frivolous enquiries of the sort you might wish to instigate."

"No relation to Abercrombie & Fitch the clothiers," Rachel added. "They are situated in Burlington Gardens, I believe."

With that they withdrew. Collapse of elderly couple. Cheers, (inaudible) from others present.

"Well, that was fun, wasn't it, lover-girl," said Alice in an aside to Rachel.

"Please do not call me that ever again," Rachel pleaded. "It is just too tacky for words."

"Sorry, love," Alice said contritely. "I was just paraphrasing what I thought was in that dreadful old couple's minds."

"Let us not go anywhere near the appalling pits of their rancid mental processes otherwise we will be contaminated for ever and a day," Rachel said firmly.

"God, you are a drama queen," Alice said, punching her on the arm as they both ran down the street towards the harbour to have another look at the boats, this being the first day there had even been a hint of sunshine. Rachel punched her back and they had a running boxing match all the way.

Saturday morning came and it looked as though the weather was clearing and they might be fortunate in finding some of the Exmoor ponies wandering around. They said their farewells to the hotel staff and one or two friends they had made among the other residents and retraced their route towards the B&B they had come across on their outward journey.

"Rita Longford said we were welcome to arrive any time today, as she's not going out," Vera reported. "She's preparing an evening meal for you fussy vegetarians though, and I think by the sound of it we're in the potato soup as well, so as long as we get there by early evening all will be well."

"Why don't we go to the caff for lunch?" Alice said. "The food was OK there and then we could go to the B&B, get unpacked and then wander off to the pony club or go far a walk on the moors if the weather holds - or even if it doesn't!"

"Anyway, we rather took a fancy to that Lisa girl," Rachel said. "She looks as if she could be fun."

"Mm, so did I," said Tom. "She'd be quite a handful, I would think."

"I don't suppose you're going to have much of an opportunity to test out your proposition," Vera said drily. "But your opinion has been noted."

"I expect this is the first symptoms of the onset of middle-aged crises," Alice remarked to the vehicle at large - they were just passing through the hamlet of Bolventnor - "but I expect there will be many more. It will all be very innocent and probably consist of a collection of simple but endearing poses of young ladies skimpily dressed engaged upon some innocent domestic task—"

"Such as dusting with a feather brush daintily held in one hand while smiling coyly at the camera——" Rachel supplemented,

"Or a pretty vignette of a maid engaged upon crochet work————"

"A waitress bending over as she pours out a cup of tea for the gent lounging at the tea-table————"

"A trim little nurse bending over a patient's bed waving a thermometer and pulling back the bedclothes————"

"Without her knickers on!" shouted Rachel as the car drew to a halt at some traffic lights. In the lane beside waiting to turn left was a police car, the occupants of which, having clearly heard the last few words, the car windows being down at the time, cast an official eye on the neighbouring vehicle. The two young people had suddenly gone very quiet. Vera wound her window fully down.

"It's a sad fact of modern life," she said conversationally to the driver of the police car, "that children nowadays have lost all sense of proportion in their activities and are also far too precocious in their knowledge of areas which had previously been the domain of adults. I suppose deportation to one of the colonies is no longer a viable solution in this over tolerant day and age?"

"I'm afraid not, madam, but I would recommend a series of cold baths and an administration of bromide to reduce the young person's fevered system," the driver responded in kind.

"Thank you, officer, an excellent idea. We shall administer the doses to them immediately we get them home and into a cold bath."

The lights changed, both vehicles moved off to their different destinations and the rest of the journey was relatively quiet in the Darwin car.

****

They arrived home later the following afternoon having had an enjoyable time with the Longfords who fulfilled their expectations of hospitality and proved to be kindred souls in their love of nature, good food and conversation, essentials for the well being of the human animal. Lisa had taken Alice and Rachel to the Exmoor Pony Centre at Ashwick and introduced the girls to the staff there who were only too happy to show them around and tell them the history of the Exmoor Pony Club and its development over the years. They left their new friends with promises of returning the following year and keeping in touch as a matter of course.

Joseph and Rebecca greeted them with open arms, a fine nut roast with steamed vegetables and a golden syrup pudding with custard to follow, and also the latest news from the village.

"Sergeant Wootton proved himself very able and has sorted out all that nonsense at the school," Joseph informed them as they sat down to dinner. "The unfortunate Roberts is being cared for in a nursing home and those boys have got what they deserved, I'm happy to say. Causten and Edwards are both in a young offenders institution and the other three boys have been put on probation. I don't know whether the school will take further steps against them, but I imagine they're on the best of behaviour or else! Also," he added, "Rachel's bluff worked and most of the possessions have been returned to their owners."

"Probably the first time a sheet of paper with nothing on it being waved in front of the crowd has had a positive outcome," said Tom drily. "We could try it ourselves one day if we find ourselves *in extremis*."

"Nonsense," said his good lady. "It's simpler to just shoot the buggers."

CHAPTER XV

When school reopened the following Monday, Assembly was buzzing with excitement and wild speculation. Alice and Rachel were besieged with questions as they walked through the school gates on that overcast and damp October morning. They fended off rumours that they were going to be expelled, made head girls (like Romulus and Remus in Ancient Rome? they teased), imprisoned, given the Victoria Cross, put in the stocks or perhaps presented to the Queen and awarded an M.B.E. They responded to demands to know whether they had been interrogated by the police, or put in a safe house, by a simple recitation of the truth. They had been down to Cornwall for a short holiday with their parents and also been to see the Exmoor ponies and were just going to continue as ordinary pupils and it might be an idea just to forget what had happened and get on with their lives.

The Headmistress delivered a short but severely worded announcement concerning the fracas on the evening of the last day before the half-term break. She reported that the two chief offenders had been expelled and were now serving a custodial sentence and that the other three members of the group who had instigated the outrage were suspended until the end of that term and were being privately coached at their homes. She added that there were strict injunctions on anyone trying to contact them, but if there was any complaint outstanding against any of the members of the gang for theft or illegal possession of an article belonging to any pupil, that would be dealt with directly by the headmistress herself. Mr. Roberts, the Assistant Headmaster, had been taken ill and was recuperating in a nursing home, therefore pupils under his tuition would be allocated new teachers and pupils should apply to the notice board for the changes in their rosters. She added that if there were ever any repetition of such a barbaric attack on any pupil, the school would inevitably come in for censure and possible closure by the authorities. She reported that there was a distinct possibility of an emergency visit from the Inspectorate of Schools and she therefore expected all pupils to behave themselves in a seemly and appropriate manner from this day forward and would come down heavily on any pupil who fomented trouble of any sort. She said that her staff were primed to be on the lookout for any evidence of bullying or favouritism and that any pupil who was being bullied could apply in complete confidence to herself or any member of the staff for help. She added that she intended to beef up the lax system of monitors and prefects which had been in place until now, and instigate a system of form monitors and senior pupils who would be responsible for their allotted charges. She also intended to appoint a head girl and a head boy with their deputies who would be rôle models as well as leaders in their field, either of sport or academia. Eventually she might even consider the election of such personnel to be decided by a democratic voting system. This brought a cheer from the assembled children and heads turned to look at Alice and Rachel who were quietly seated at the rear of the room. They modestly looked at their hands.

Finally, the Headmistress relaxed her stance and heaped praise on Rachel and Alice for their stand against the bullying tactics which had been displayed by the gang, but added that there was to be no repetition of the actions taken that day to disarm and confound the miscreants. She impressed upon them that such actions only worked once and when the element of surprise was taken out of the equation, the gesture could very well rebound to their disadvantage. She reminded them of the classic story of Godiva, Countess of Mercia who rode through the streets of Coventry naked except for her long hair covering her, as a protest against her husband's egregious taxation of his tenant farmers. The Headmistress pointed out that in the nine centuries since that event, nobody in the world, as far as she was aware, had repeated the act to this day. Until now, that is, she added. This brought the house down or rather up because nothing could contain the outburst of jubilation which followed that statement. A swirling mass of children jumped up and descended on the two girls who were then carried in triumph on the shoulders of a cheering mob down the stairs of the school and out into the playground where they were given three rousing cheers and placed on one of the lunch tables that ran alongside the edge of the playground.

"This school is becoming more like St Trinians every day," one of the younger teachers commented as the staff followed the mob outside, amused but also rather overwhelmed at the spontaneous wave of affection and support which flowed from the children. Amelia was quite awed at the response.

"I had no idea they would respond like that," she exclaimed. "It's quite amazing, but at the same time I have no intention of imitating Mr. Alistair Sim's portrayal of the headmistress!" She watched the scene with a proud feeling. Such good natured creatures, she thought happily.

"We'll let them have their heads until the third session of the day at 11.15 when I shall expect everybody to be in their places and settled down to their work. Enough time has already been expended on this matter, but no good will come of trying to bottle it all up too soon. I hope those two will be able to calm everything down now."

"It certainly looks like it, Headmistress," Evie Protheroe, the English teacher said. "Look, they have already got down off the tables and are mixing with the other children. I do think they are managing to calm them down." And indeed Rachel could be seen giving Anna, their tall supporter, a friendly hug, and there were hugs all round from many of the boys as well as the girls for both of the friends and the crowd seemed to be breaking up already.

"It looks as if we might be able to start very soon, Headmistress," said one of the other teachers. "Perhaps we ought to be getting to our classrooms now."

"Quite right, Miss Green, off you go and if you can see any of your class, please collect them as you go." She clapped her hands and soon had the attention of the whole school.

"I think we could make a start on our lessons now, don't you, children," she suggested firmly. "There will be plenty of time for you to get together in the breaks. I would be pleased if you would make your way to the notice boards and just make sure you are going to the right classroom. We have changed very little of the roster, but one or two pupils may find that they have been shifted to another class. If any of you have problems with that, it can be discussed and adjusted later if you are unhappy with any of the arrangements. For the moment though, please go along with it so that we can start the second classes of the day and get back to the essential business of the school."

The children were content enough to make their way indoors and Rachel in particular felt some relief that she would soon be more or less out of the limelight and back to normal again.

The school year rolled on and soon the dramatic events of the past few days were behind them and becoming only a faint memory in the minds of the young people and their teachers whose every hour was occupied with much more practical matters than the shattered hopes of an unhappy middle-aged man and a group of loutish adolescents.

Christmas came and went. Anna MacVitie was appointed Head Girl and Alice was appointed her deputy. Rachel had of course been approached but asked to be exempt from the honour as she felt that Anna, who had been at the school since she had been a new girl four years previously, was the better choice not only because of her character but also her seniority. Privately the Headmistress agreed but felt obliged to offer the post because of the surge of popular sentiment which had arisen over the incident just recorded. Both Alice and Rachel became prefects as they were both in the fourth by then. A sixteen year old boy named Robert Newcomb, a bright and intelligent lad who was also a good all-round sportsman was appointed Head Boy. Regular monthly meetings were introduced in order to keep everybody on their toes, and the system looked as if it was going to keep on working very well. Came the Christmas break and Amelia had good reason to feel proud of herself and her command of the loyalty and smooth-running of the school.

A school inspector had paid a visit shortly after news of the incident had reached the ears of the authorities and found a smooth-running and happy institution with creative and lively staff and pupils. He was most impressed.

"Headmistress," he said diffidently over a cup of tea in her office after his prowl round the school and his examination of teachers and pupils picked at random during the day. "The jade Rumour has told me false. Your school is in the most excellent state of affairs. Rarely have I seen such a general high standard from all sides. I had been given the idea that this was a school in need of remedial attention. Nothing I've seen today could be further from the truth. Tell me truly, how did this come about?"

"Well, Mr. Baker," said the Headmistress comfortably. "I'm afraid I am to blame for that, if anybody is. The truth is that some weeks ago, just after term began, I had the misfortune to be carted off to hospital with peritonitis. Most unpleasant." She took a sip of tea. Mr. Baker nodded understandingly.

"I can well imagine," he said sympathetically. "But did you not have a Deputy Headmaster who would have been able to take over for you in such an emergency?"

"Of course I did. Jeremiah Roberts, a most experienced teacher and excellent administrator. He had been seriously considered for the post of Headmaster at the time I was also applying for the post. It was a very close call between the two of us, but I was their choice. He should in fact have been their first choice," (Amelia Fairweather wondered at this point whether she would go to Hell for this disingenuous mangling of the truth), "except that he was not a very well man at the time. He informed the Governors of his condition, which had only come to light since his application, and begged to be scratched from consideration for the appointment at the last moment after consultation with his doctor.

"Sadly," here she paused to offer her visitor a refill of his tea-cup and replenishment of the biscuit plate while she wondered how far she could carry this embellishment of reality without breaking into hysteria. "Sadly," she continued, "when I was taken off in the ambulance, I left the poor man with no option but to carry on as best he could in spite of being in no fit state to fill my shoes. Consequently, things soon fell apart. I had not been in the position long enough to establish failsafe protocols in case I was incapacitated; Mr. Roberts was in dire distress and we had a number of young teachers who did not have all that much experience and nobody to take over with a firm hand. We also had one or two delinquents who had been warned that they would be expelled if they caused any more trouble. They took the opportunity to make mischief and terrify some of the younger children and frankly things looked bad for a time. I only learned abut this state of affairs when I came back from a short convalescence to find that anarchy reigned." She sighed regretfully.

"How did you manage to save the situation?" Mr Baker was eager to know.

"Not by myself, I assure you," she replied honestly. "I was still weak from what had been quite a serious operation. Fortunately we have some very good pupils here, a number of them are quite outstanding not only academically, but also outstanding characters in their own right. Our Head Girl and Head Boy are two such people who we are very lucky to have as pupils and a number of the younger pupils have much character and are looked up to by the other girls and boys, so we have a good thread of excellence running through staff and pupils. The new teachers are all blossoming and finding their feet and earning the respect of the students as you have probably found in your examination today."

"I have indeed, Headmistress. But what of Mr. — er — Roberts, is it?"

"He is recovering very well indeed," she lied hopefully, having had little information regarding the present condition of her Deputy Head. "I am confident that we will see him return to us next year. Such a popular master with the children." (Might as well be hung for a sheep as a lamb).

The inspector, not being a stupid man and having gleaned the essentials of the happenings at the school before his visit, considered it prudent to accept this version of events, blatantly misrepresented as they had been. He was genuinely surprised and impressed by what he had seen of the school that day, and as it was within three weeks of the resumption of classes after the mid-term break, he was also amazed that everything seemed to be functioning so well. This he put down to the Head's strength and determination to put right all the previous wrongs and also her loyalty to the school itself and everyone associated with it. He also thought that she was correct in her estimation of a number of exceptional pupils without whom he doubted she could have achieved so much loyalty and goodwill in so short a time. There had obviously been much work and effort behind the scenes to achieve this state of affairs and the inspector left with a conscious desire to pay another visit the following year to see how the school had progressed. He was assuredly going to return a high recommendation in his report to the Inspectorate. His only misgiving concerned the absent Deputy Head. He hoped the present incumbent would be able to keep him in check if indeed he did return to his post.

****

Shortly after the Spring term had commenced, the Headmistress received news of her Deputy's condition. He had been released from the nursing home with the proviso that he agree to daily visits from a carer and arrange to have a live-in housekeeper who would cook for him and keep an eye on his medication. The nursing home had arranged with a Mrs. Wilkins, (she who may be remembered as the very selfsame silly old chatterbox Mr. Roberts had overheard in the newsagent's shop relating the events of the now infamous confrontation all those months previously), to live in as housekeeper and cook for the patient. In spite of her undoubted propensity for gossip, the lady was at the same time a good hearted and competent person who would make sure that her charge was well fed and properly looked after until such time as he was fully independent again.

The Headmistress was dubious about approaching him, however, as she was uncertain how such a move might be countenanced. Her husband recommended that she offer a tentative invitation on neutral ground, such as the village tea-shop at a weekend when she did have some leisure time. After a decent interval after his return from the nursing home, she sent him a greetings card with an open invitation should he so wish to join her for afternoon tea whenever he wished at a convenient weekend. His reply was prompt and courteous and they agreed to a rendezvous that very Saturday afternoon. By then it was the middle of February and the weather, though wintry was not unpleasant.

She almost did not recognise him at first as he walked into the teashop. Gone was the horrid little moustache, his hair was closely cut and although it had lost some of its colour, looked healthier and cleaner than the last time she had seen him. His skin colour had improved greatly and he seemed to have shed many years of stress and incipient bad health along with the grim and unyielding expression of former years. He smiled charmingly at her and they shook hands before sitting down in the corner of the café which the headmistress had chosen as the most neutral of all neutral areas.

"My dear Jeremiah," she exclaimed, genuinely warmed by the presence of the person sitting in front of her, "how well you are looking. I hope you are feeling as fit as you appear!"

"Yes indeed," he replied cheerfully. "Somewhat bolstered by some mild medication it has to be confessed, but generally I am fitter then I have been for years. I now have a good hour or so of brisk walks twice a day usually and I manage to get a swim at least a couple of times a week at a public baths which entails a bit of a drive sometimes but gives me an excuse for a day out which is very pleasurable. My good fortune is that I have enough private means to be able support a leisurely existence. I hadn't realised how much I needed it!" The waitress reappeared at that moment with tea and cakes.

"What a nice little tearoom this is," he added, as the waitress left the table. "Do you know, I don't think I ever realised that it was here!" Amelia smiled at him.

"It sounds as if a new life has opened up before you," she said encouragingly, pouring him out a cup. "What do you feel about resuming teaching? Do you think you might come back to the school?"

He looked very thoughtful for a moment. "I don't think," he began slowly, "that anybody, including myself I might say, would think that a good idea at the present. Personally I am enjoying my freedom and have put all thoughts of career on hold for a while. It may even happen that I may get married before the end of the year and I have no need, for the time being anyway, to earn myself a living."

"That, I think, is most sensible of you," she replied. "Without doubt the teaching profession has much to recommend it, but it is not without its stressful components."

"How tactful you are, Amelia," he said. "I must tell you that, with the help of some truly wonderful staff at the nursing home, I was able finally to face up to my behaviour last year and to account for it, if not exactly with honour. but at least with an understanding of how little self-awareness I possessed. Without such amazing proficiency and genuine kindness on the part of the staff, I would not be reconciled to the events that took place and my own lack of responsibility with the welfare of those children. That also goes," he added firmly, "for my lack of responsibility to those boys. To have encouraged them in such egregious behaviour was, and still is, inexcusable. I think you probably realise that it is far too soon for me to contemplate a return to your school or even a career as a schoolteacher."

His words struck a deep chord of sympathy in the headmistress and she understood that he had, in fact, crystallised the misgivings that lay at the bottom of her judgement about her erstwhile teacher's suitability to continue in his chosen career. She looked at him with a new respect.

"You have obviously become a good judge of your own abilities and potential," she said. "When you mentioned the possibility of marriage, I take it as a possibility that you met someone in the nursing home to whom you have become attached?" He laughed quite openly.

"Yes of course," he admitted. "How often is it that a patient becomes enamoured of his or her therapist and saviour? It's perfectly understandable and of course labeled as transference and sometimes quite a problem for both the therapist and his client. Fortunately in this case, one of my saviours was a very pleasant and kindly nurse and I think I can say that Helen and I became mutually pleased with each other. I am, by nature anyway, no hero worshipper and she is eminently sensible so there is no question of adolescent infatuation involved."

"You are to be congratulated, both of you, and I do hope it turns out well for you both. In that case, reverting to the question of your future, what do you have in mind, or am I being too presumptuous in asking that of you?"

"No, no, my dear Amelia. Not at all. You have every right to know what intentions I may have formulated about my future and certainly inasmuch as they concern my association with the school. I think it would be better all round if I distance myself from the school entirely for the moment. You will have to find yourself a new Deputy Head and I will have to settle my mind to a different pathway. May I talk to you, do you think, concerning my childhood, not in any great detail, I wouldn't want to burden anybody with any of that," he protested, "but just a general idea of my upbringing?"

She poured them both out some more tea and said, "Of course you may, if you think I am the right person for any confidences."

"Well," he began, taking a particularly large meringue from the plate of cakes with which he busied himself while collecting his thoughts about his childhood. "My mother died when I and my sister were both very young. It was sudden and more than possibly affected my father in a very negative way. I think he probably blamed the two of us, especially me, for his wife's sudden collapse and death from meningitis, because although I have only a hazy recollection of him before that event as we were mostly with our mother and rarely saw him, I only became aware of his hostility after her death. He was a schoolteacher himself and had been on the staff at Harrow and was determined that I should follow his profession. My sister, of course, was only fit to become a wife and mother as far as he was concerned. She defied him and when she was old enough took off, and I have completely lost touch with her. He was somewhat like Mr. Barrett of Wimpole Street and just about as intolerable, now I look back at my youthful years. I never intended, you see," he said sadly, "to become a schoolteacher, but that seemed at the time to be the only possible career for me. Oh, I think I made quite a good shot at it, but obviously over the years, my frustration grew and festered and I started to make the most elementary mistakes in my attitude towards my pupils. I expected them to treat me with a deference quite out of any reasonable expectation and so the more I expected their obedience, the more they despised me."

"Is your father still alive?" she asked gently.

"Oh no, "he replied." He died some years ago. Heart failure, the surgeon said. He was in hospital for some minor surgery and died under the anaesthetic."

There was a silence between them. Of course, Amelia thought, his pupils' attitude reinforced his own self-loathing and so it went. A crisis occurred and he was then forced to admit his dilemma publicly to his therapists or to accept the consequences of his actions and face a jail sentence. The challenge ultimately seemed to have freed him from the awful burden of the past and opened up a new and happier future for him. She sincerely wished him well and assured him that he was, in actual fact, a very good teacher and he would be wise to keep that ability in reserve in case he ever found a need to return to the profession. She was also secretly relieved that he had come to this decision. If in the future he was settled and in a different frame of mind, she thought he might even enjoy it and forget that he had been coerced into it by his father, but that would have to wait for some distance to be put between the leaving of it and the return.

"So, did you have no idea what you really wanted to do when you left school? Had you no ambitions at all?" Roberts laughed and his face lit up like a schoolboy's.

. "Oh yes, I had a good idea of what I wanted to do, such a very good idea!" He chuckled. "I knew exactly what I wanted to be, but it was of course completely impossible. With a father who was unimaginative, intolerant, xenophobic and biased in particular to all things American, I really had no chance of realising my ambitions." He smiled reminiscently. "I wanted to be a jazz drummer," he said simply and rather sadly. "I wanted to be another Gene Krupa, a Buddy Rich or a Mel Lewis, an Art Blakey, any of those great drummers, but I'd have been content just to play in an unknown dance band just for the pleasure of playing. However, I never had the courage to even broach the subject with my father. I knew he hated jazz and any popular music. He'd got as far as Verdi in his musical tastes and that was his limit. Anything further than that was total anathema and the work of the devil!"

"So are you now going to learn to play the drum-kit?" Amelia asked with a smile. "Oddly enough I happen to have a friend who teaches drums. Henry and I sometimes go up to London for a night out at Ronnie Scott's and have the occasional visit to a jazz festival here or abroad. We're both very fond of jazz and it's what brought us together all those years ago. We actually met at Ronnie Scott's." She smiled at his amazed expression. "Would you like me to give you an introduction to our friend?" she said. "I can guarantee he's a first class musician and a great drummer. He's more or less retired from regular work now but he used to be a session musician and he's played for almost all the greats at one time or another."

"Oh, Amelia would you," he was almost beside himself in ecstasy, but then his face clouded over. "What if I'm hopeless? I've never had a chance to find out whether I have any talent at it and I'm really a bit long in the tooth to break into that world."

"Well, this is true of course," she said cheerfully, smiling at him. "But I wouldn't let that put you off. Remember Grandma Moses? She started painting when she was 76 years old and lived to be 101! Not quite the same as drumming I admit, but nothing's impossible unless you believe it, so you might as well just go for it. At the least," she added, "you'll have some fun doing it."

"Well, why not indeed? You are so right, Amelia and I am so happy that we had tea together today. You've really inspired me to just enjoy myself and have a go at it. I won't know whether I'm any good by just sitting thinking about it, will I!" They both laughed and Amelia wrote out the name of her friend with a contact telephone number and handed it to her companion.

"I suppose I had better get myself a drum-kit first of all," he said a bit doubtfully. "I'm not really very knowledgeable about makes or anything really."

"Don't do anything until you've been to see Terry," she said. "He's a very sensible and reliable person and will advise you about what you should get as a beginner, and if he thinks you have any ability or talent he will advise you properly. He's a very nice man and I'm sure you two will get on well together. As you see, he lives in Bristol so you won't have to travel too far if he takes you on for regular lessons. He'll be able to tell whether you've got any sense of rhythm quick enough and also if you've got enough coordination to handle a drum-kit and he'll tell you straight away, so put your trust in him."

Roberts agreed to do just that and they parted happily from each other, he going off with a spring in his step. She just hoped that he wouldn't be disappointed if her drummer friend turned him down. As she made her way homewards her mind turned once more to the seemingly perennial problems of the successful running of her school in a country where the Government of the day was in seemingly total disarray with disastrous educational policies, some of which were doing great harm to the education system. She had managed, with a mixture of obstinacy and cunning to withstand the stream of conflicting diktats and changes flowing down from Whitehall which threatened the mere survival of many institutions. She had even managed, while still only an English teacher at the same school to provide free milk for the needy children of the parish in the face of the niggardly and foolish Thatcher's ban on free milk for schools and her meddling as Education minister under Heath's government in the early 70s. The following administration hadn't shown much ability to either change anything or preferably, to stop tinkering with the system and so, with a cunning and ruthlessness belied by her gentle demeanour, she kept her school and its inmates in good educational health. Her present problem was finding a domestic science teacher of quality. Her dearly beloved Mary Barnes, who had taught generations of children to cook and fend for themselves in the kitchen, had passed away during a particularly cold and bitter week earlier that month. Admittedly she was 83 years old although she would never confess to being a day over 59. "They'll be sure to try and retire me," she would confide to her close friends, "and then what would I do with myself? Oh no, I'll go on until I drop in the cooking pot one day – won't that be a nasty surprise for someone!"

Domestic Science was a particular favourite of the Headmistress. She was of the opinion shared by many, that to be able to cook oneself and one's family and friends a good meal, was almost like writing a symphony and just as valuable. It also discouraged people from buying the junk food that was so readily available and with such ruinous effect on their health. It should be noted that, in the face of repeated requests from salesmen to install drink dispensers on the school grounds, both her predecessor and she had forbidden any such drinks being allowed on the premises. Fizzy drinks from American proprietary brands were expressly forbidden and warning notices placed on the school notice board about the unhealthy aspects of such foodstuffs. There were also lectures on the subject as part of the curriculum and consequently the general health of the school was very high indeed. She thought she might ask her friends, the Darwin and Katz families of they had any ideas on the subject.

CHAPTER XVI

The following day Amelia and Henry Fairweather arrived at the Darwin's house in response to an invitation from Vera the previous evening and in time for eleven o'clock coffee. Vera greeted them both at the door.

"Tom's just refereeing a bout of hand stick fighting which the girls have been practicing recently,"she explained to them. "They've been at it for twenty minutes already and we thought they would have been done by the time you arrived but you're welcome to watch or not as you please. It shouldn't last much longer, I don't think. Anyway, come into the kitchen and you can watch it from there."

The Fairweathers followed their host into the kitchen and saw the two girls standing relaxed and facing each other outside in the garden. In their hands they held rattan sticks about two feet long and Tom was explaining something to them. He then stepped back and the pair began sparring first of all quite gently but steadily increasing the ferocity of their attacks until Alice, with a deft blow, sent Rachel's stick flying over her head. Without missing a beat the defenseless girl had leapt at her opponent and brought her crashing to the ground. Alice lost purchase on her stick and the two of them were grappling ferociously. One moment Rachel was on top and apparently strangling Alice who would then break the hold and heave Rachel off her, rolling on top of the now prostrate girl with her arm across her neck and temporarily in control. Rachel then managed to kick backwards and catch the other girl in the back of the head. This only encouraged Alice to strengthen her grip on her friend's neck, who immediately tapped the ground beside her in submission. Alice stood up and helped her opponent to her feet who immediately wrapped her arms around her and gave her a resounding kiss on the lips. The two girls then sauntered towards the kitchen looking mightily pleased with themselves and with their arms around each other, Alice taking her father's hand in hers as they passed him.

"Thank you, Papa, for refereeing us," she said.

"Who didn't collect their equipment?" Tom demanded. "Sorry, Papa," they said and Rachel went back to pick up their rattan sticks which she handed to Tom. In the kitchen Vera was recounting how they had been known as Tweedledum and Tweedledee when they were barely two, not only because they agreed to have a battle, but also because they used to stand like that with their arms draped over each other's shoulders looking remarkably alike.

The Fairweathers had watched with amazement and alarm the contest between the two girls. "Surely," Amelia protested, "they should be wearing some protective clothing for that sort of activity?"

"Not really," Vera replied unconcernedly. "They're very lightweight sticks and they hardly ever land a blow and then only lightly. They never hurt each other much, you know, and then so rarely as to be no more than a passing bruise or scratch. What they are doing is to practise evasive and defensive action if they are ever attacked by somebody with a stick or other weapon of that nature. It's only when they do Kendo that they have to wear full body armour and they've only just begun on that."

"They're very skilled, though, aren't they?" Henry said admiringly. "They're so fast and such energy. Amazing, really. Have they been practicing martial arts for some time now?" Vera laughed.

"They came out of the womb practicing martial arts," she said, as the two girls came through the kitchen door with Tom following and carrying their sticks. "Hullo, Headmistress," they greeted their friend. "Were you watching us having a fight?"

"And most impressive it was, too," Amelia said appreciatively. "I don't think either of you have met my husband, have you? Alice and Rachel, may I present my husband, Henry, who will now also be one of your devoted admirers." Both girls shook hands with Henry and excused themselves to go and have a shower as they claimed to be totally unfit for respectable company in their present post fight state.

The adults settled down to coffee and a discussion about the Head's quest for a domestic science teacher. Vera said that she had a teaching degree and would be willing to help but she could only spare a couple of hours a week and then only intermittently as she could not guarantee to be home for long stretches at a time. Amelia explained that they were having great difficulty replacing Mary Barnes and had had no support for the subject from the education authorities. Alice and Rachel came downstairs looking demure and virginal in their white dresses which they wore for special visitors. Amelia's eyes sparkled with amusement. "You don't fool me, you know," she said pleasantly. "Either of you!" The two girls looked at their headmistress with wide-eyed innocence. "I can't think what you mean, Headmistress," Rachel said in a mock hurt voice. "Are we not pure and innocent as the driven snow? Would not butter not melt?"

"Driven slush, more like," Vera said coarsely. "And I'm not so sure about that double negative neither!"

"I believe they put butter inside the mouths of the recently dead at one time just before burial to ensure that the corpse really was a corpse." Henry offered this piece of gratuitous information out of a combination of slight embarrassment and considerable mischief. The children looked at him with polite incredulity and everybody broke into laughter, including Henry.

"Right, kids," Tom said, "You both look very sweet and would you like some coffee and can you help solve your headmistress's problem concerning a domestic science teacher."

"Yes please, and possibly yes we might be able to," Alice responded. Tom poured them each a mug of coffee and handed it to them. "Until you find somebody suitable to replace Mary, would you like us to take the domestic science classes? Basically they are about cooking and we're both pretty fair cooks, wouldn't you say, Mum?" She looked across at her father. "Dad?"

"We do have one or two free periods," Rachel added, "and come to think of it, I would actually enjoy doing a bit of cookery teaching. We can also give tips on cleaning ovens and how to use the basic pots and pans and other kitchen utensils." Amelia considered the proposal.

"How would you be about discipline?" she asked. "Keeping pubescent children focused can be quite a problem sometimes even for very experienced staff, you know." She wondered as she came out with this caveat, whether it also applied to these two as well!

"We're both prefects, Headmistress. Push comes to shove there's always the sink and a cold water tap," Alice said firmly. "I don't really think we would have too much trouble there unless we prove to be absolute duffers at teaching. If that proves to be the case, we'll give up immediately but I think we would start off with at least some cooperation from most of them."

"I'll think about it," she agreed. "I'm extremely grateful for your suggestion and your offer, don't think I'm not, but there may be some problem about the legality of the situation. I really have every confidence in you," she said sincerely. "And thank you again for the offer."

"When did you learn to cook?" Henry asked them. "Or perhaps I should ask you when did you ever find the time?"

"When they weren't busily gouging each other's eyes out, you mean?" said Tom laughing.. "I'm not sure. When was it, girls?"

"It was at one of our birthday parties; I think we were about six then," Rachel said. "As we were born within two days of each other, I was born on August 21st and Alice on the 23rd, somehow we decided between us to have one big birthday party for the two of us on August 22nd,"

"Right on the cusp of Leo and Virgo," Alice added.

"So we get the best of both worlds you see!" Rachel said.

"It surely doesn't work quite like that, does it?" Amelia protested. "You can't just change your birthday to suit your favourite star sign.

"Oh, I don't know," Alice said smugly. "Works for us!"

"So you learned about cookery on this composite birthday," Henry said placatingly. "How did that come about?"

"They had some of their little friends round for the whole day. They'd usually came round just after breakfast, about a dozen of them, and it was almost always sunny at that time of the year so they were fortunately outside in the garden having a riotous time, but on this occasion I hadn't got anything ready for the day for some reason," Vera related.

"We'd just got home the day before," Tom said, "and Rachel's parents had had to go off to a conference that very evening after dropping the kids, so we were lumbered with a garden full of voracious little people who would be screaming for nourishment very soon and only an elderly tin of mixed biscuits and some home made lemonade between them and starvation."

"We couldn't even find the magnificent birthday cake which Rachel's mother had baked and then hidden away from their predatory hands."

"So we all made lunch together ———-"Alice said,

"From scratch - all of us kids," Rachel completed.

"We took the whole party over to our vegetable patch and picked greens, dug up potatoes and carrots, picked fruit, until we had enough of everything and then they all helped to wash the veggies, peel the potatoes and cut them all up and we made a wonderful stew with hard boiled eggs in it somewhere, mashed potatoes on the side, and I think all the kids enjoyed the making of it almost as much as the eating of it." Vera grinned at the memory.

"That wasn't the end of it though was it, Mum," Rachel said. "We all contributed to the steam puddings which we had later on. I can remember having a great time with the flour and melting the butter and stirring it all up in the huge basins we had then."

"And learning how to make custard!" Alice added with relish. "Yum!" she giggled.

"We've still got those huge basins but they just won't seem quite as big now you've grown, is all." Tom said. "I think that must be when they got interested in cooking. Certainly they're a dab hand at some dishes and even invented a double-decker pizza which has got to be tasted to be believed."

"That was me," Rachel said modestly. "One day I thought I'd like to make a pizza and do it all from scratch, get the right flour, mix it all up, twirl it round and all that stuff you see them doing in real pizza bars, prepare the fillings and basic sauce which I did, but then discovered that we hadn't got a pizza tray."

"Horrors!" exclaimed Amelia with well simulated astonishment, "So what did you do then, you clever creature?" Rachel eyed her warily while the rest of her audience smiled broadly.

"Well, land's sakes and Heavens-to-Betsy! What could I do but use a regular baking tray?" Rachel managed a fairly good imitation of one of the characters from 'Little House on the Prairie.'

Amelia clasped her hands and widened her eyes in well-feigned admiration. "Oh my!" she breathed. Henry looked at his wife disapprovingly. Tom and Vera were rocking with silent mirth and even Alice had a secretive smile on her face.

"But then," Rachel paused dramatically. "When I had laid down the pizza dough, spread the sauce and laid all the variety of tinned artichokes and olives, peppers, hard boiled egg slices and other delicacies on it, it looked so empty that I covered it with another layer of dough and spread sauce and a different variety of veggies on top and then finished it off with the grated cheese, popped it in the oven and it was sheer heaven and aren't I just as clever as clever can be!" She fluttered her eyelashes at them. They all gave her a round of applause and Amelia said she thought it was a wonderful creation, but she was considering returning Rachel to the second year stream at school owing to her infantile behaviour.

****

"Well, that seems to have solved that problem at least temporarily," Amelia said to Henry as they walked home. "Aren't they just terrific, those two? Mind you, I think it's down to the parents as well. They treat them as adults and not children, so they have learned a responsibility towards themselves at an early age."

"Why do they both treat the Darwins as their natural parents? It's a bit odd the way Rachel calls Vera 'Mum' and Tom 'Dad'. Does Alice do the same with the Katzs?"

"Oh, yes," his wife replied. "I think it's because both parents looked after the children when the others were away on business so they grew up with two sets of parents each. A novel idea really."

"Well, they're certainly a revelation, but for all their sophistication and intelligence they're still children though. I notice they fool around and giggle just like other kids of their age."

"Well, of course they do, Henry. Real people never grow up. All the best ones remain enchanted children all their lives, just like you and me, in fact!"

Henry turned towards his wife and clasped her in his arms, and to the amusement of the few inhabitants abroad, gave her a resounding kiss.

"Well, there go our reputations," said the satisfied lady happily.

"About time, too." agreed her uxorious husband.

The Headmistress's insistence on Domestic Science as a regular subject from the first year of schooling meant that both Alice and Rachel had a good idea of how to go about instructing the novices as they had been through the same procedure themselves. They had their first experience of class teaching the following week when they were presented with twenty-six first year pupils crowded into the school kitchen. If they wanted to use the kitchen they had to have their cooking lessons either early in the day before the professional cooks needed to start preparing lunches, or the last sessions when everything had been cleared away. To get things moving, Alice and Rachel got the children to roll their sleeves up, wash their hands and put on aprons and their paper hats. For the first lesson, they got their class to prepare and roll out pastry, make sure it was properly done and then line the baking dishes for the readily prepared filling which would then be covered by a top layer of the same pastry. This required quite some preparation before the class started, so that each child had a good go at kneading and rolling the flour to the right consistency and getting the feel of the dough as it was worked. It took a surprisingly long time for the beginners to do this elementary chore and by the time the large baking dishes had been lined with all the individual contributions, the pre-cooked fillings (usually meat and vegetable) in place, the upturned china chimney placed strategically in the dead centre of the dish and the covering layer of pastry laid carefully on top, it was time for them to put the dishes to one side and clear up the resultant mess on the table, sweep the floor, wash their hands and rolling pins, remove their aprons and fold up their paper hats for next time. All being well, the dishes would be finally baked for that day's lunch by the kitchen staff and the next lesson might consist of preparing the meat and vegetables as well.

That was all very well for the beginners but the girls had to face some more serious challenges with some of the older children who were, thanks to Mary Barnes' enthusiasm and love of cooking, very advanced in culinary preparation themselves. They just managed to keep ahead of the game but it was quite a close call sometimes. On one or two occasions with the fifth and sixth forms, they bowed to the superior knowledge and let the pupils have their heads. If it looked like getting out of hand, they always had the Indian curry card to play with. This was a facet of Mary Barnes' instruction which was non-existent, but both Alice and Rachel were able to make a very respectable Biriani and some tasty curries. After one failed attempt at instructing 5b in the art of a crepe suzette, the next week they came prepared with a wide range of herbs and spices and that day the school was treated to a superb vegetable curry and rice which re-established their credentials. Fortunately that Easter, a full-time domestic science teacher was appointed who could also stand in as supply teacher in case of need.

    Both girls were relieved because, much as they had enjoyed the challenge, it was taking up a lot of their leisure time which they rather needed for other pursuits. Amelia thanked them both very warmly. She said she thought that she might be fighting a losing battle with what she described as that Grocer's Idiot Daughter's notion of being Minister for Miseducation. She foresaw dark days ahead for education generally and sadly she was proved right, but that is another world which need not concern us at this point in the narrative. Something much more inimical was lying in wait for the two girls and young Timmy Henson.

CHAPTER XVII

The school had finally broken up for the Easter vacation on Friday, April 1st, All Fools' Day. Young Timmy Henson and some of his friends had scampered off into the woods to play. Sunset was just about on the dot of 8.00 that evening and they had stayed out late and had had themselves a riotous time with games of hide and seek and Martians and Earthmen and anything to prolong the glorious freedom of no more school for at least a fortnight! Timmy and his friends parted company some way from the main road as his house was at the north-eastern end of the village which was out of the way for the other children. The light was still fairly good though and he should have seen the rabbit hole on the edge of the path but he was tired and a bit dreamy and he didn't. The consequence was that he twisted his ankle most painfully and had to sit down and recover from the shock as it had made him feel quite sick for a few moments. He whimpered gently to himself for a moment or two, but he was a brave little boy, as we have discovered, and he picked up a sturdy looking length of branch which he found fortuitously close to hand, and using this as a crutch, made his way homewards slowly but painfully. He found he had to stop every few yards, however, as the pain was getting quite severe and he only had the strength to proceed in short distances before he had to stop and rest against whatever support was available. He had just about reached the main road when two things happened. A cloud came over what was left of the evening light and Alice and Rachel came across him as they were returning from their evening run. Rachel examined the swollen ankle gently and pronounced it badly in need of treatment as she thought it possible a ligament had been torn and he needed professional help. He was very relieved to see the two girls because by that time he was almost fainting from the pain and distress.

"Hang on in there, Timmy," Alice said comfortingly to him. "We'll carry you home and make sure the doctor comes round to see you immediately. Your parents will be back by now, won't they?"

"No, nobody's home until late on a Friday," he said miserably. "They leave my dinner for me ready to heat up in the oven when I get in, because they're always so late from work." Alice looked at Rachel.

"Perhaps we should get him to the hospital first," Alice said. "It's the other direction but if we take it in turns to carry him, we'll get there in fifteen minutes at most and they'll have a doctor or nurse or ambulance if necessary. So up you come, young Tim," and with that she picked him up and over her shoulder in a fireman's lift and they started walking towards the cottage hospital. There was very little traffic on the road at that time which was a relief in one way and the cloud had passed so they had some twilight; they also had a soft verge to walk on most of the way. They had been going for only a few minutes and Alice had just transferred Timmy onto Rachel's shoulder when the sound of a motor vehicle made them draw into the side of the road. It was a small white 5cwt van and when the driver saw the two girls walking along with their burden, he slowed down and his passenger wound down the nearside window.

"Hello," a friendly voice said. "Do you need any help?"

"Our friend here has twisted his ankle very badly and we're taking him up to the cottage hospital in the hope that there may be someone there to help him."

"Oh dear," said the friendly voice. "Do you know, I think that the hospital has just been closed down, and anyway it was only really a maternity hospital, you know."

"We should do as we were both born there," Alice said laughingly. "What do you suggest, then?"

"Well, why don't we take you on to Exeter where there's a proper Accident and Emergency facility. We can always bring you back afterwards if they can't supply transport for you."

"That's extremely kind of you," Rachel said. "But isn't it out of your way?"

"Heavens no," said the voice. "We live there so it's no trouble at all and I can see the poor little fellow's not at all happy." This was certainly true as the poor little fellow had fainted with the pain. The passenger door opened and a small stout clean shaven man with a round merry looking face stepped out of the van.

"You just pop in here," he said, opening the rear doors. An interior light came on and they saw that the inside was furnished with a bench seat facing the front of the vehicle. "If you lay your little friend along the seat and sit at either end of him - you will have plenty of room, you see - then you can make sure he doesn't roll off onto the floor, but my brother will drive very steady all the way and we'll be there in a tick, won't we Adrian?" he addressed his brother who had also got out of the driver's seat and come round to help install the passengers in the back.

"We will indeed, Cedric," said his brother. They both had rather high pitched sing-song voices which Alice thought could very well become irritating with too much exposure. However, this was just for one journey. What could possibly go wrong!

The rear of the van was isolated from the driver's cabin and the two men shut the back door on their passengers and climbed back into the front. The van moved steadily off and the two girls sat in the back of the van with their charge. The light had been left on and they began to feel very sleepy possibly due to the motion of the van and being in such an enclosed space with no windows. A warning thought had begun to cross Alice's mind just before she lost consciousness. Her last memory was of Rachel who had obviously fallen asleep herself and had rolled off the seat and was lying sprawled on the floor.

****

When Alice began to regain her senses, she discovered that she was lying on a bed set against a wall in what she thought was a converted cellar. The walls had been white-washed and there was a single unshaded 40watt bulb suspended from the ceiling. The room, or cell, was no more than six by four feet and about six feet between ceiling and floor. She lay as still as she could after her first reaction on waking and examined her surroundings through half-closed eyelids. There were some sounds coming from an adjacent area but they were very muffled and she was unsure of their origin. A door opened nearby and she heard a snatch of conversation, then that door was closed and a lock was turned in the door of her cell. The door was opened cautiously and the head of one of the two brothers appeared round the door.

"Are we awake, then, my dear," the sing-song voice enquired and Alice gave a little whimper as if she had just woken.

"Where am I?" she quavered unoriginally in a tremulous voice. The man edged cautiously into the room. Whether it was Adrian or Cedric was immaterial to Alice. She knew exactly what was going to happen to whichever one of them it was and shortly after the brother would be dealt with in a similar manner. The man approached the bed and sat on the side of it.

"Now, my dear little girl," he said coaxingly, "we just have to make a little examination to find out all about you, nothing for you to be worried about, but please don't struggle because then I'll have to ask Cedric to come in and help me and that wouldn't do at all, would it?" He reached for the top of her tracksuit trousers. Alice withdrew her legs and curled up into a ball.

"Please don't hurt me," she whined. "Where's Rachel? I want to see my friend. I want my Mummy," He sat back and regarded her with a conspiratorial smile on his face.

"You want your friend do you?" he said. He leaned over her. "What little naughties do you and your friend get up to, eh?" He placed his hand on her bottom. "Do you play with each other's little cunnies, do you? I bet you've got a lovely little minge just like your friend has and I bet you lick it and play with each other with your fingers, don't you?"

Alice decided to put an end to this before he got himself further aroused. She gave a frightened gasp and drew back against the wall and as he leaned into her she punched him hard in the throat. He staggered back and fell off the bed. She swung her legs off the bed, swaying slightly from the after effects of whatever gas they had pumped into the rear of the van, but managed to kick him soundly in the ribs over his heart. He passed out and she made her way to the door and found herself in a cellar space at the bottom of a flight of stairs leading up to what she surmised was the ground floor of whatever building they were in. She closed the door quietly and turned the key which was in the outside of the lock. She didn't think anybody could have been alarmed by what had just happened as Adrian, whom she deduced it was from what he had said, had been able to make nothing but a strangulated gurgle when she had attacked him. She took her bearings and saw that adjacent to the room she had just vacated was another door with a key still in the lock. She put an ear to the door and could hear the singsong murmurings of brother Cedric as he no doubt was trying to woo her friend into submission. She opened the door very carefully. Cedric had got further with Rachel than his brother had with her for the very good reason that Rachel was still under the influence of the soporific. He had managed to remove Rachel's tracksuit trousers and underpants and was busily engaged in parting her legs so that he could examine his victim's private parts in close detail. So absorbed was he indeed that he had no notion of what caused him to black out completely as Alice delivered a two-handed rabbit punch to the back of his neck. She managed to drag his inert body clear of the bed and Alice tried to revive her friend by gently administering slaps to her face alternating with chaffing her legs and hands. This appeared to be leading nowhere and Alice was getting very worried that not only might the man regain consciousness, but that Rachel was immobile and she couldn't manage to get both her and a wounded Timmy out of this hell-hole by herself. And where the devil was Timmy anyway? Had they dropped him out of the van or disposed of him somehow? Was he still alive?

And then, seeing her friend's naked lower half, a memory of an acupressure point, the perineum, midway between the anus and the vulva which, it was claimed, could be stimulated to galvanise somebody whose heart had stopped. Well, this might be totally idiotic but she reckoned it was worth a try. The result exceeded all expectations. Rachel's eyes flew open suddenly as Alice was stimulating the area, and sitting up smartly with a gasp, demanded to know what the fuck was going on. Overriding her quite understandable demands for explanations as to her strange location, her state of undress and need to know her whereabouts and what had happened to Timmy, Alice urged her friend to dress herself immediately and follow her out of there. Alice locked the door behind her but left the key in the door and they crept up the stairs. At the top was a wooden door which they opened cautiously to find themselves in the hallway of what appeared to be an ordinary terraced house. Facing them was the front door and freedom, the other way led to what they surmised was the kitchen area from which they could hear a low-pitched crooning sound. Compelled by necessity to find the little boy and rescue him from his present predicament, they crept toward the glass door only a couple of feet from where they had emerged from the basement. They opened the door gently to be confronted with the rear view of the largest person that they had ever seen. She must have stood a good six and a half feet and weighed a probable 28 stone if not more. She was bending over Timmy who lay stretched out on a sofa which occupied one wall of what was obviously the eating area of the large kitchen beyond which they could see a glass hothouse with some suspiciously tall grasses in pots.

The gigantic woman turned a large moon-like face towards them and looked almost surprised to see them although the face was so uniformly blank of any articulate passion or expression that it was difficult to tell what was actually being registered in the mental processes, if any, behind it.

"Hullo," Alice said in as friendly voice as she could muster. "We came up to see if Timmy was OK. Cedric and Adrian asked us to come and check on him." She smiled winningly at the woman. The mouth opened very slowly.

"Aw," it said. " 'Ave they finished playing with you then?" she said slowly. "They don't usually stop once they're get going."

"No, but this time they were worried about Timmy, you see," Alice explained slowly and clearly to the creature. "And they thought if he wasn't too well, we should take him up to the hospital, you see."

While this conversation was plodding on, Rachel had been examining Timmy. She caught Alice's eye and gave a partial thumbs down signal. Alice said firmly,

"Cedric and Adrian told us to take him to the hospital if he wasn't better, so we'd better go now. They asked you," she continues slightly desperately as she saw the cogs beginning to turn in the woman's head, "to put the kettle on for tea." she added somewhat hysterically. Meanwhile Rachel had gathered Timmy up in her arms and moved towards the door.

"Go on," she said firmly to the woman. "Do as you are told or those boys will be very angry with you!" This had the desired affect and the woman suddenly lost the belligerent light that had begun appearing in her eye at the intervention of the two strange people in her kitchen and her normal subservience had taken over. As she turned to obey the instruction a faint banging sound could be heard from below. Alice and Rachel with her burden made their way briskly to the front door. It took one or two heart stopping moments to undo all the bolts and then they were out in the street. Alice shut the door behind them and turned to see what number the house was.

"So, number 12 and what's this street?" They walked towards the brightest end they could see. Alice made a note of the street name and they looked round for some evidence of where they were.

"Glory hallelujah!" Rachel said nodding her head across the more brightly lit road they had reached. Alice laughed out loud, "Thank the Lord," she said. "A taxi firm." They made their way over and entered the cigarette smoke filled cubicle. There they got something of a shock. When they asked for Exeter General Hospital, the cab controller was puzzled.

"You got any particular reason for going all that way?' she asked. "We've got a perfectly good A&E here. Musgrove Park."

"This isn't Exeter?" Rachel said amazed. "Where are we then?"

"Taunton, my dears, Taunton." The controller said. "Look, is it for that young lad you've got in your arms?"

"It is indeed," said Alice. "We've been badly misled and he twisted his ankle seriously some time ago so we really need to get him seen to as soon as possible."

"Tell you what, I'll ring the ambulance for you. That way you save a fare and they'll be able to deal with him immediately and save a bad jolting around in one of our old cabs. They're all out at the moment anyway, it being closing time, you see." She was as good as her word and an ambulance arrived within ten minutes of her 999 call. Meanwhile Alice asked if she could use the public phone as she wanted to make a reverse charge call to talk to her parents.

"You come on in," said the friendly controller. "You can use this line here and you'll be a bit more private." They both thanked her and Alice phoned home while Rachel nursed Timmy who was still unconscious but looking very white.

Alice spoke to her father, who told her that there was already a hue and cry for the three of them and he was very relieved to hear from her. She explained what had happened in guarded terms and gave the address of the house in which they had found themselves and the possible state of one of the men in the house. He said he would contact the relevant authorities immediately and also the Hensons. He told them to wait at the taxi firm as he was on his way with Vera to pick them both up.

Alice had been very elliptic in her report but the controller had sharp ears and was an ex-policewoman who understood very well the general import of the conversation.

When Alice finally put the phone down and turned to thank the woman, she said, bluntly, that if what she had understood was correct, then the girls had hopefully achieved what nobody else had managed to do for the last five years and that was to find the answers to the disappearance of several young people. Timmy was being attended to by the ambulance men who wanted to know what had happened to make him lose consciousness. Rachel was explaining to the ambulance driver and his female partner that they had all three of them been gassed but they didn't know what had been used. At that moment two police cars pulled up outside the taxi firm. A policeman appeared at the door of the ambulance. "Are you Alice?" he asked. Rachel told him who she was and that Alice had just come out of the taxi station and was standing behind him. "Do one of you feel up to accompanying us to this address?" he asked them. Alice said she would go with them as Rachel wanted to stay with Timmy as he would no doubt be very alarmed when he woke to find only strange faces around him. Alice and Rachel gave each other a hug and unashamedly kissed each other which amused the cab controller but slightly shocked the policeman. The ambulance then drove off to Musgrove Park and Alice gave a brief description of what had happened at the house they were driving towards and what thy might expect to find on arrival. She calmly admitted that it was possible she had actually killed one of them, but at the same time felt little or no regret. The officer, never having come across this attitude in one so young before decided to withhold judgement until he knew exactly what the situation was.

On arriving at the premises they could hear a tremendous hullabaloo in progress. The front door was wide open and Cedric, or was it Adrian? was outside the door shouting and screaming while inside they could just discern the figures of the giantess and Adrian, or was it Cedric? in violent altercation. The officer strode into the building, his men deploying themselves suitably, two of them trying to contain the violently ranting Cedric (Adrian?) and the rest of the contingent following their leader and Alice into the house.

"Now then! Now then! Now then!" cautioned the officer to the quarrelsome couple. "What's going on here?" The pair rounded on him. Adrian (Cedric?) shouting that he couldn't enter without a warrant, the gigantic female, being more practical, rushing at him and bowling him over by sheer weight and kinetic energy. As she came flying out of the door after her prey, Alice, who had been following the officer, put out a foot and tripped up the Leviathan who, with a scream and resounding thump, fell flat on her face onto the street completely knocking the wind out of her sails and any wits she might have had fleeing well out of her or anybody else's reach. The officer picked himself up with Alice's helping hand, thanked her quietly, and with the help of a number of his men, bundled the two miscreants into the back of the Black Maria which had just rolled up. The other brother had wound down by now and was squatting on floor of the rear open door of one of the police cars nursing his throat and chest.

"I think that must be Adrian," Alice said quietly to the policeman. "I punched him in the throat and kicked him in the heart. He seems to have survived," she said with a touch of regret in her voice.

"As has the other one," remarked the officer. "What did you do to him to allow him to live as well?"

"Double handed rabbit punch to the back of the neck," she replied. "I thought I heard a decided crack as he went down, though. Anyway," she added cheerfully. "I'm glad really, otherwise I suppose I might be had up for manslaughter which could have been a bit of a nuisance."

"If you would kindly wait in the car, miss," he replied noncommittally, "we'll make sure you get home all right."

Alice told him that her father would be along soon to take her home and was he sure he didn't want her to come into the house with him and point out the scene of the crime and give him all the details. He assured her that he was in no need of further assistance but was very grateful for her help so far and thought the best thing for her would be to sit in the quiet and wait upon the arrival of her parents. She thanked him, climbed into the rear seats of the nearest police car and immediately fell fast asleep.

"Well now!," mouthed the officer to himself in admiration and, taking a rug from the boot of the car, covered the child with it. He then went into the house to start a search of the premises. What the police discovered is not essentially part of this story and so I will not burden you with the appalling and horrifying results of their search of the premises including the walled garden to the rear of the building. Strange to relate but no mention of either of the girls' or Timmy's part in the downfall of the brothers and discovery of the remains of a number of young people in that infamous house in the Somerset town was ever revealed publicly.

CHAPTER XVIII

Tom and Vera had collected the Hensons *en route* to collect their own children and then take them on to the hospital to see Timmy. The police had discovered the van in the garage at the side of the house, which had a door leading directly into the rear part of the kitchen. They had also found the cylinder and were able to give the information to the hospital so that the three youngsters could be medicated to relieve the effects of the gas. Alice woke to find herself in her father's arms and being transferred to another ambulance which had been summoned at the request of the police who were concerned for Alice when she had fallen asleep so quickly. All three children were subsequently treated for gas poisoning and it was daybreak before the Darwins arrived home. Both girls had slept heavily in the back of the car and had been put to bed where they stayed until the following morning having slept non-stop for 24 hours. Timmy had remained in hospital and his parents had elected to remain with him until he was fit to return home. Happily it was the weekend so there was no conflict of work obligation to add to their worries. It turned out that Timmy was awake and comfortable enough to return home on the Sunday afternoon, much to everybody's relief.

That Sunday afternoon the Darwins had a visit from the police officer who had led the raid on the house in Taunton. He introduced himself as David Jennings. He was an experienced officer who had spent some years with the Met and then moved west to join the newly formed Avon and Somerset Constabulary, which meant an advancement in his career as well as a welcome change of scene for his family.

"My wife is a Bristol girl and she hankered after her home county especially when our first baby arrived. These sort of cases though are always pretty harrowing and too near home for any policeman's liking," he confessed. "I just thought I would call to thank both your young ladies for their courage and the way they dealt with those villains. They were in a very dangerous situation, especially as they had to consider their young friend who needed treatment."

"I expect you would like to see them," Tom said as he welcomed the policeman into their kitchen. "Have a seat and I also expect you could do with a cup of tea – or do you prefer coffee?"

"Tea's my tipple," David said pleasantly. "How are the young people?"

"Well, they slept all through Saturday, got up about 11.00 this morning: we had brunch, and then they went back to bed again and we haven't heard a peep out of them since. I expect that gassing has had a more lasting effect than we reckoned on. I want Rachel's parents, both of whom are medical people, to have a look at them. Unfortunately they are away at the moment but should be back tomorrow. If not, I'll take them back to A&E. They seemed very competent and nice at Musgrove Park, I thought."

"And how's the little boy doing?"

"As far as I know he's OK. It's maybe fortunate he was out of it for most of the time, but his ankle is healing well, I think, but nobody knows what's brewing in his mind. He's quite a reserved little person, a bit like our two, but at least they have each other for support. Timmy's a bit on his own but his parents are decent people. We'll have him round for a day when he can walk again comfortably."

"So Rachel's parents are away?"

"Yes, I think they're attending some conference somewhere. Unfortunately it's not always easy to get hold of them at a moment's notice."

Vera said, "I'll go and see if those two are in a fit state to come down and say hullo, seeing as how you've made a special journey to visit us." She left the room on her errand.

"Rachel?" enquired David. "She's not your daughter, then?" Tom laughed.

"No, she's the daughter of our good friends Joseph and Rebecca Katz. People get a bit confused but both the girls have grown up treating each of us parents as communal property because we take it in turns to look after them both when one set of parents is abroad or off on business somewhere, so it works out like that. Also, of course there's only two days difference in their ages and they've grown up together and are equally important to all of us."

The policeman thought that he perhaps understood enough of the relationship between the two girls not to press for any more details. Vera returned to the kitchen saying that they would be down shortly and were very pleased that the officer had called.

"They're very well behaved when they're not punching somebody's lights out," she said, grinning at their visitor. "We teach them lots of things, but they do seem to have a natural appetite for scrapping and defending themselves, which is just as well." She looked at him seriously. "How bad is this business, really?" she asked.

"Quite terrible," he replied bitterly. "I don't want to go into too many details, but we have found enough hard evidence to convince us that many of the missing children over the last five years have now been accounted for."

"Dear Christ," Vera muttered under her breath. "What possesses these people?"

"And what of that female?" Tom asked. "What was her relation to those two men?"

"Apparently she was one of their first victims while they both still at school. She was a local girl, a simple creature, whom they bullied and abused. It was a case of a victim becoming so attached to her persecutors that she more or less fell in love with them. Perhaps it would be better to say that they somehow enchanted her into being their sex slave. After they had left school their parents died in a car accident and bequeathed them that house and quite a bit of money. They inveigled this unfortunate creature into coming to live with them and look after them as housekeeper, cook and general factotum and bedmate except when they felt the need to go on the prowl when she acted as guard dog for them. Your two girls were very lucky to have bamboozled her into letting them go. I would really like to hear their account of what happened that night."

"We would also be interested to hear that too, because they haven't said much about it up to now!" Vera said. She poured some tea out for her visitor and persuaded him to some of Rebecca's wonderful Dundee cake. Alice and Rachel came downstairs hand in hand and looking still a bit sleepy-eyed. They were introduced to their visitor and Alice thanked him for his consideration with the blanket in the police car.

"What would you like us to call you?" Rachel asked him. "I don't think we can address you as 'Officer' or 'Mr. Policeman' do you?" He laughed.

"I'm a visitor, please call me David," he said. "and I'll call you by your given names if that's acceptable!"

"Sit down and behave yourselves," Vera snapped. "All these airs and graces! Anybody would think we were in a Jane Austin novel."

"Tush, the idea!" exclaimed Alice sitting down and smiling sweetly at their visitor. "I think we've been more affected by that wretched gas stuff than we know," she said seriously. "I don't think we've ever slept for such long periods before, except when we had chicken pox one year."

"I wouldn't be surprised," David said. "The elder of the Crutchley brothers, Adrian, was a trainee anaesthetist. They both had connections to the hospital. Cedric was a porter there and they managed to nick a number of tanks of the right components and customised their van very cleverly so that anybody in the rear compartment could be rendered unconscious within a very short space of time, Of course it wasn't very professional or controlled as it would be in the theatre, but it served its purpose and the victims didn't usually last long enough for any miscalculations to matter."

"You mean that they've actually been poisoned and it's going to take a while for the bad effects to wear off," Vera said bluntly.

"I'm afraid so," he replied. He looked at the two girls. "If your medical parents haven't returned by tomorrow, I suggest you go straight back to Musgrove Park," he said to them.

"We will," Rachel said. "I hope they'll be back by then but sometimes they get delayed. We've never got completely used to it. Shall we tell you our story now? I expect there are some details which you need to know about, but I don't think either of us is going to be able to stay awake for too long and I'm very sorry because it would be good to discuss the whole business with you and get it out of our systems. Don't you agree, love?" She stretched out her hand to Alice who took it and gave it a squeeze.

"OK, shall I start?" Alice said. "Can I have some more tea please, Mums," she said, passing her cup over to Vera. "Me too," added Rachel.

They settled back in their chairs and, having taken a slice of cake, between them they recounted their whole adventure up to the moment David Jennings stepped out of the police car at the taxi station. They were good at narration and told their stories accurately and pithily and without embroidery. The policeman in David Jennings was impressed and thought that they would make very good witnesses, but he was aware that it would be better all round if they did not appear at any of the hearings. If they did, they would have to be heard *in camera* and the press would have to be excluded. Jennings thought that they had enough evidence to put away both men without revealing too much of what had transpired before the public ruckus which the police had come across when they drove up to the house.

"There is one thing that intrigues me about this affair," David said, when they had finished. "What would you have done if this woman had turned on you? She's three times your size and weight and like many huge people she can move very fast when she wants to."

"A bit like the rhinoceros in fact," Alice said. "Gets up to 60 miles an hour from a standing start in about three seconds."

"More or less," he smiled at her. "But seriously, what would you have done?" Rachel looked thoughtful.

"I don't think she had much confidence really," she said. "When I was firm with her she was just obedient. I think if she had challenged us, we could have challenged her back; to go down to the basement and find out for herself whether we were telling her the truth or not."

"You do realise that she had never been down those stairs, don't you?" David said to them. "That is, until the other night in response to the brothers banging on the doors in the basement."

"No, but that would have been part of the power we had over her, providing of course, that we didn't panic."

"I was actually getting a bit hysterical myself," Alice said. "When Rachel got firm with her I felt a real sense of relief. I didn't want the confrontation to escalate because then we might have had to subdue her somehow or even stick a knife in her which would have been quite horrid and I think I'm exhausted sorry I'll have to go back to bed now." Tears had sprung to her eyes and she got to her feet a bit unsteadily. Rachel was at her side immediately and Tom and Vera stood up in order to help the children upstairs. Rachel seemed to be coping quite well with the unhappy girl and with a general apology to the company and especially to their guest she helped her friend upstairs.

"Should someone sit with her tonight?" David enquired of her parents.

"It's all right," Tom said placidly. "She'll be well looked after. They've slept in the same bed all their lives, except when they were at their worst with the chicken pox and then they had single beds in the same room. They're very mutually supportive."

"That I can see," David said. "She's in shock still and might need a bit of counseling, wouldn't you think?"

"We'll get them over the effects of the gas poisoning first, I think, but you're right. Hopefully Joseph and Rebecca will be home tomorrow who are pretty good helping people with stress caused by wars and the dreadful things people do to each other."

"Would you care to stay and have a bite to eat with us?" Vera asked him.

"You're most kind, but I think I want to get back to my family. It's my only bit of free time until after the next weekend, so I want to make the most of it. I would like to visit again though, and I hope both those girls recover quickly. They've had quite a horrible ordeal. Just being in the same room as those two wretches is enough to curdle anybody's stomach. It has mine, I can tell you."

"Did they say how much they loved their little friends and only wanted them to be happy in Heaven?" Tom asked him. David held up his hands in horror. "Please, you sound as if you were there!"

They said their goodbyes and David said he would call in on the Hensons on his way home and wondered whether Timmy might benefit from a chat with Rachel's parents as well. Tom said that he had already suggested it to them and it could all be arranged discretely once Timmy was recovered.

When the policeman had left, the parents went up to the girls' bedroom. Vera tapped gently on the door and Rachel, who had been sitting beside her unhappy friend propped up with pillows, opened the door to them.

"She's very mis," she said simply. "I expect it's not being helped by the anaesthetic we were both exposed to. It's a wonder we managed to keep awake long enough to get out of that terrible house. Poor love," she stroked Alice's head. Alice took her hand in hers and kissed her fingers.

"I don't know what's going on with me," she said sadly. "I don't seem to be able to stop crying. Why is that?" she appealed to her parents who had sat down on the bed beside them.

"It's shock, sweetie," Tom said gently. "And also I think you're right about the anaesthetic. It's still in your system and affecting you chemically. Don't fight it, it'll pass."

"Why don't I bring you up something light to eat?" Vera said. "Another pot of tea for you both and some cake and a few sandwiches unless," she added, "you would like a cooked meal? If

I start now, I could knock you up a spaghetti or a risotto pretty quickly."

"Thanks, Mum, but tea and cakes and a couple of sarnies would be great. I think anything cooked would be a bit too much for me at the moment." She sniffed.

"I don't usually get like this, do I?" she appealed to them. "I mean, Rachel's not snivelling away like a two-year-old is she, yet she was in just as much shit as I was."

"Hey, don't start beating yourself up, Alice," said Rachel. "I was completely out of it until you had dealt with those two men. It was you who really rescued us all, you know. I'm not surprised that you're in shock," she added. "If you hadn't taken it all on your own shoulders, we'd probably be dead by now. Oh God, I'm sorry, love," She clasped Alice in her arms as the tearful child broke into heartrending sobs. Vera and Tom put protective arms around both the children, their eyes moist from the empathy that flowed between them.

"Sorry, darling, I shouldn't have said that," Rachel murmured. The sobbing eventually died down and Alice sat upright in the bed and rubbed her hands over her face. The others drew back gently to give her some room. "What I need is a jolly good run and then a jolly good swim and then a jolly good fight and then!" she leapt out of the bed. "A jolly good———"

"ALICE!!!" they all shouted in unison. Everybody froze and they stared at her.

"A jolly good cup of tea," she said innocently.

"That child!" Vera expostulated as she marched out of the bedroom and went downstairs to put the kettle on and cut some sandwiches. Tom smiled at them.

"Good thinking, my dear," he said to his daughter. "Glad you've got your priorities right." he followed his wife down the stairs. Rachel and Alice rolled about on the bed together and canoodled happily for a while. Then they got up and Alice went to have a shower while Rachel tidied herself up and went down to join the adults in the kitchen.

"We're both suddenly feeling much better, but I don't know how long that's going to last. When will this stuff get out of our systems?" she asked them.

"No idea, really, but I wouldn't have thought more than a couple of days at the most." Tom said vaguely. "I mean, alcohol metabolises quite quickly really and I imagine gas has some similar volatility, wouldn't you think?"

"You haven't the slightest idea what you're talking about, have you?" his wife said crossly.

The next day saw the return of Joseph and Rebecca. They were appalled at what had happened in their absence.

"Thank God, those children have been brought up to defend themselves," Joseph said. "It horrifies me to think that so many young people have no idea what to do when molested by such monsters."

"Some societies do rear their children to be fighters," Tom said, "but they live in truly dangerous parts of the world. Here we're cushioned from predators which is why we have the police and the army to protect us. Like many facets of our society there is an element of illusion."

"Well, they're certainly getting a good grounding in double-dyed villainy in this quiet little corner of England." Vera said grimly.

"Remember what Sherlock Holmes said about the countryside!" said Tom.

Rebecca had a quiet word with the children and confided in the Darwins senior that she did not think too much harm had been done. If anything the experience would prove useful to them as they were both extremely resilient and also capable of understanding the motives which led some people to becoming predators and villains. She also considered that, for instance, Alice's distress was mostly due to the gas poisoning, but she had obviously been exposed to more stress than the other two and consequently was reacting more. She thought that it would be sensible to keep a sharp, but unobtrusive eye on her for a while. Rachel, sensing her mother's concern, said that she would be particularly mindful of her friend's welfare and would take care not to upset her if she could help it. "Although it's pretty difficult to know what does upset the mad little creature sometimes!" she remarked petulantly. "Come along, darling," Rebecca said soothingly. "You know you love her and remember, we all have different levels of tolerance and sensitivities which are not always very apparent to others, even those we love deeply and with all our being,"

****

Both girls had worked the poison out of their systems by the middle of the week; Timmy had not been so fortunate. For one thing he was smaller but had received the same dosage as the girls. Also he was laid up with a swollen ankle which, in normal circumstances would have healed quicker, but the delay in getting him to a doctor and the effects of the anaesthetic had impeded his progress quite severely. Being unable to engage in any of the usual activities of a normal eleven-year-old, he also became a bit depressed. The one good thing was that he had been unconscious for almost the whole time, so there had been little opportunity for him to experience any of the naked fear which a realisation of his predicament might have caused him. It might even have saved his life, as the Crutchley brothers had abandoned him to the care of their watchdog Rosa, while they eagerly set to work on their other two more appetising victims.

Consequently, his days were occupied with reading and playing board games with his parents in the evenings, when they were home, or with the two girls and his large friend, Anna. Anna had organised a roster of care for him while his parents were at work. She had just been told the bare bones of the ordeal, but gathered enough to realise that the three children had indeed been in considerable jeopardy. She proved herself again a stalwart friend to them and willingly gave her time to being Timmy's principal carer while Alice and Rachel were also recovering. She got the loan of a bath chair from a friendly neighbour and Timmy at least got some fresh air and congenial company. When the two girls had recovered sufficiently, they invited Timmy and Anna and a few of their other friends round to the farm-house for a day of fun and games which cheered the little boy up a lot but certainly left Alice and Rachel somewhat exhausted and their parents quite frazzled. They also managed to get Lisa Longford and her parents to drive over from Exmoor for the day.

"Never again!" Vera swore, when the last child had finally left. "Oh, go on,!" Alice said. "You loved every moment of it, you know you did. Who was it started that game of French cricket and got so involved that she knocked the ball into the next field and it took a quarter of an hour to get it back from the doggies!."

Vera plonked herself down beside her daughter on the settee and pulled her close to her. Rachel came over to sit on her other side. Vera wrapped an arm around each of them. "You are right, of course," she said, happily. "We all had a lovely day and it's such a joy to have the house filled with kids, even though they're screaming and yelling and carrying on like demented ferrets!"

Tom came in from clearing up some of the mess in the garden to find his wife and the two children fast asleep on the settee in each others arms. He went into the hallway and extracted his camera from the small chest of drawers that stood by the hat stand. He took a couple of snaps of the idyllic scene which used up the roll of 35mm film. He'd taken any number of pictures of the day's events and considered that these last two were a fitting tribute to the end of a perfect day.

CHAPTER XIX

A few mornings later and just before the start of the summer term the two friends woke to the sunshine pouring into their bedroom. Alice rolled over and threw an arm round Rachel. "You awake yet?" she asked softly. "Mm, just about," she replied sleepily. "What's the time?' she propped herself up in the bed to have a look at the bedside clock. "Ooh, ten to six," she rolled on top of Alice and they rubbed noses. "Shall we go for a run? And then we could have a Kendo practice. Do let's," she said. "At least we could practice getting kitted up and if Tom's awake he could give us a lesson or get kitted up himself and take part."

"I've been thinking, Rache," Alice said. "Why don't we start giving WuShu classes for some of the kids. Beginner's stuff, you know. I bet that would go down well with them and it might be real fun teaching it. I mean, we're reasonably advanced by now, aren't we"

Rachel lay sprawled across her friend. She thought about it for some moments. "Well, I think that could be fun. Why don't we first ask Dad and then, if is OK with him, we'll talk to Choo when we go for the weekend training and see what he thinks."

"And then we'll ask the Head if we can do it after school one day a week. Come on. Race you to the bathroom." So saying, she pushed the other girl off her, leapt out of the bed and made for the shower.

The following weekend was the last before the summer term: it was also the bi-monthly master class given by the WuShu master Choo which was held in Exeter. He suggested to the two girls that they might be ready to start their classes within a couple of years when they were older and had had some more experience. He agreed that they both had enough skills and ability to set up the classes now but that they would have problems with school authorities and also there was not only the question of their teaching certificates, but they would also have to be insured. It was getting increasingly difficult to set up any business without insurance on account of a burgeoning interest in litigation by the general public. If anybody so much as fell over a slightly sunken paving stone, some lawyer was ready and waiting to start proceedings against the relevant council for negligence. It was becoming quite a profitable business and many small companies, osteopaths and similar individual practitioners were having to increase their charges because of the exorbitant premiums being demanded by insurance companies. Only recently the Post Office had been successfully sued by a foolish woman who, carrying too many parcels kept in place by her chin, had stumbled across an item of Post Office furniture and had fallen and cracked her elbow. In spite of the fact that it was plainly her fault for not looking where she was going, her claim for compensation for damages and disability in her profession, (freelance orchestral percussionist), was successful and she was awarded over £70,000 by the court, the Post Office having failed to mount any degree of argument in their defense. (If they had known that the same woman had been playing at a concert at the Royal Albert Hall the previous Sunday, they might have challenged the claim more effectively. Unfortunately, nobody told them).

Choo suggested that they work for certificates in physical education as well and when they were old enough, they could apply for a position either at the school or start up a business on their own. He knew that they were disappointed but consoled them with the notion that they could always have their own private sessions with any of their school friends and also there were many routine training techniques for building stamina and reflexes which would not be injurious.

They talked it over with their parents and with Amelia one weekend when she and Henry came over for tea, and were unanimously advised to wait until they were at least sixteen before thinking about it again. Amelia did say, however, that it would be an excellent idea to incorporate a certain amount of martial art training into the P.E. classes. All they needed was an instructor with those skills!

"I think it's good that they're showing a thought for their future," Rebecca said to Vera over morning coffee that first morning the girls had gone back to school. "At least they have an idea that one day they might have to earn a living for themselves."

"I don't see either of them becoming full-time teachers, though," Vera said. "Not that they couldn't, but I think they'd get pretty bored once the novelty wore off."

"I expect you're right," replied Rebecca rather sadly. "They did very well with the cookery though, didn't they."

"Oh yes. Amelia was very pleased with them, but the sun is inclined to shine out of their little bottoms as far as she's concerned, whatever they do."

"Understandable really, considering."

"Oh, yes of course. I think she loves them almost as much as we do. Thank God she's sensible and discreet enough not to show it in public."

"What do you think they'll do with their lives? Do you think they'll follow in our footsteps?"

"Hope not, really. Wouldn't wish that on anybody. Probably obliterate all trace of us in the process!"

"Seriously though; Rachel I'm sure will follow some sort of science career which would be a good course and I see Alice maybe going in for linguistics and semiotics, something to do with languages anyway. I don't think either of them have a leaning towards medicine or horticulture, do you?"

"Not really. I reckon they'll become ninja assassins actually. They really are quite lethal, both of them, in their charming way."

Which is about as far as the two mothers got in their speculations about their children's futures and as it turned out they were not far out in their prognostications.

The years passed and both girls reached the end of their secondary education with the qualifications for University entrance. Neither of them where interested in a University education however, and opted for what has now become known as the gap year. This simply entailed leaving school at the end of their sixteenth year and taking occasional employment at the Darwin's market gardens and the Bedford Arms. It enabled them to contribute to the expenses of both households and also have some pocket money and time for their own pursuits. Their good friend Anna had gone to Cambridge to read Ancient History and Timmy had suddenly shot up and was now a respectable 5'11" in his stockinged feet. Both Alice and Rachel had outgrown their innocent seeming and childish looks and were turning into strikingly beautiful young women. It didn't impair either their sense of fun, nor indeed was their passion for each other or sense of duty in any way diminished. They were still essentially the same brave spirits that had been evident the day they were born.

Amelia Fairweather's school went from strength to strength and Anne Martin, the P.E instructor took her Aikido black belt and incorporated some elementary aspects of the discipline in her regular classes; Alice and Rachel also ran an evening class once a week in WuShu which was very well attended. Of Jeremiah Roberts there was little news until the Fairweathers, on one of their weekend jaunts to London, had happened on a small combo playing at the Boar's Head at Barnes, which was known to be a favourite venue of Humphrey Lyttleton and his band. If they had not been approached by the drummer during a rest between sets, they would never have recognised the slimmed down and totally bald man who had been keeping the quartet together so skilfully.

"Thought it was you," he greeted them, delightedly. "You're having one of your naughty weekends, aren't you!"

"Great balls of fire!" Henry exclaimed in his precise banker's voice. "Jeremiah Roberts, if I'm not mistaken." Amelia for once was speechless.

"Shush! Jerry please," pleaded the drummer. "I'm Jerry Robb now. I'm afraid Jeremiah Roberts is a person of the past." Amelia found her voice at last.

"Well, this is a lovely surprise, and what a good little group this is. I like your pianist very much. A touch of the Oscar P. about him but why not. So Terry thought you had some promise then!"

"Terry gave me a new life," he said gratefully. "He took me under his wing, let me have a room in his house and coached me for a year before he ever let me loose with another player, and since then I've never looked back. And all thanks to you, my dear Headmistress!" He gave her a hug. "And how's everything at Milford St.Evelyn? And those two extraordinary children, are they still at your school?"

Amelia explained that they had just left, having passed all their final exams with flying colours and taking some time off before deciding what to do next. She didn't tell him of their unpleasant experiences in Taunton and remained noncommittal about their doings as she felt, probably wisely, that this was a subject best not brought up however much the ex-deputy headmaster had found a new life and vocation. He told her that he and his nurse had finally got married and they were both very happy, (well he was, at any rate, they would have to ask Helen about that!} and were now living in Shepton Mallet. She was still working as a psychiatric nurse and often came to listen to him play but tonight, unfortunately, she was working. As they drove back to their hotel after a very pleasant evening Amelia remarked that the salvation of Jerry Robb and his rebirth were one of the crowning achievements of her life.

"Not," she added modestly, "that I did anything but recommend him to go and see Terry and, of course, managed to persuade Sergeant Wootton to give him the option of treatment instead of prison."

"I think you can give yourself a little pat on the back for that, my dear," her loyal husband said.

Only a few weeks after the actual event which Amelia had not thought wise to mention to her one-time Deputy Headmaster turned jazz drummer, David Jennings had paid the girls' families another visit as he had promised, mainly to bring them up to date on the fate of the Crutchley brothers and their unfortunate slave, but also to see how the girls were faring. Cedric and Adrian had been committed to Broadmoor for life. They had been examined by psychiatrists and found to be criminally insane. Rosa had been assessed as educationally subnormal with a serious thyroid imbalance and had been placed in a special needs care home.

"So far, so good," he concluded. "And you both look as if you'd recovered well from your experiences."

"Oh yes," Rachel had said. "Once the effects of the anaesthetic had worn off, we were basically fine again. My parents are both psychotherapists to add to their impressive list of medical accomplishments," she smiled wickedly at her parents, "and they got inside our heads and mended a few broken synapses, especially," she clutched her friend close to her, "this poor demented little creature." She heaved a long theatrical sigh. Alice fluttered her eyelashes demurely at the policeman.

"Wasn't there some business at your school last year with some of the older boys?" he asked them innocently. "A sort of challenge I heard it so described by my colleague in the village."

"So you've had a word with the estimable Sergeant Wootton?" Joseph said gently.

"Yes, I called in as a courtesy to let him know I was on his patch. He was very discreet, but he did say that some serious trouble had been averted by the prompt and courageous actions of two of the second year girls. Quite a revelation apparently and he was most impressed." He looked straight at Rachel. "He said something about one of them undressing herself to demonstrate some argument she had with those boys, but I expect," he continued after a slight pause, "that the story is apocryphal and grossly exaggerated." Alice and Rachel looked at each other blankly.

"Was that the little set to we had with Causten and Edwards, do you think?" Alice said with a straight face.

"Storm in a teacup," Rachel said blandly. "You know how these things get blown out of all proportion." She turned to David. "Village gossip. They've nothing much else to think about most of the time." He appraised her speculatively.

"But didn't it end with those two boys landing up in approved schools and another three being barred from school for the rest of that term?" he pressed them gently.

"I think we heard something to that effect," she said vaguely, "but of course we were busy with our schoolwork and didn't have anything to do with that part of it."

Vera took a deep breath and puffed it out again with vigour. Rebecca looked meaningfully at Joseph.

"I thought," Tom said urbanely, "at one time that Alice, the product of our loins," here he bowed to Vera, "was the more malignant of the two young harpies you see before you, but obviously I was in error." He paused as both young people assumed a hurt and almost tearful attitude and looked pitifully at their visitor. "In fact, I think you must share the blame here," he looked directly at Joseph and Rebecca, "for spawning this limb of Satan and releasing it upon an innocent and unsuspecting world."

"Aw shucks, Paw," Rachel whined. "I dun no bad stuff. I'se a good girl I is."

"Enough, for God's sake," Vera said. "Why on earth do you have to set them off like that? They'll be above themselves now,"

"Beside themselves with hubris," chimed in Joseph,

"Sliding backwards with deceit," from Tom,

"Cackling with meretriciousness," from Rebecca,

"And underneath ourselves with humility!" Alice said and the girls giggled and the adults laughed and this time David Jennings stayed for a meal.

****

A few years later, in a small conference room in Whitehall, the rather likeable but mercurial army colonel whom Vera and Tom had met in Falmouth was conferring with a small circle of his colleagues.

"What do we think about those two girls in Devon?" one of them enquired. "How old are they now? Getting on for eighteen? What are they up to nowadays?"

"They're marking time at the present, I would say," volunteered the colonel. "The odd job, here and there, helping out the Darwin's business, barmaids at the pub, that sort of thing."

"Keeping up with their training, are they?" another of the group asked.

"Oh, yes. Regular morning runs, usually ten miles or so. Our resources are limited but they check every so often and get reports from the parents. Kendo practice with the Darwins senior and regular attendance at WuShu. In fact, more so since they have more time on their hands. I'm told they're not neglectful of their academic studies either."

"The way they dealt with those Crutchley brothers was amazing, I thought," said the one who had brought the matter of the girls up for discussion. "Are they just as effective now, do you think?"

The ex-colonel laughed. "Doubly so, I would have thought. Those two charming young ladies, and I mean they really are delightful, are also very determined, courageous and in my estimation quite lethal. If any of you haven't seen the film that Joseph Katz took of the incident at the school I suggest you have a look at it. That should reassure you concerning their capabilities."

"What about boy friends?" one of them asked. "If they are so alluring they must have any number of young, and not so so young, lads wanting to get in their knickers."

"As far as that goes in the village, their past history of dealing with the male sex has done nothing to encourage approaches by any of them. They are, according to Jack Hamilton who owns the pub where they work sometimes, invariably polite and friendly to the customers, but have the ability to send shivers of fear travelling the length of the spine of even the most drink-sodden hopeful."

"A useful accomplishment," murmured one of them.

"Do you recommend that we place them with Lucy Davison at Finishing School, then?"

"We can but try," he cast an amused glance over his colleagues.

"What's the difficulty?" asked the other.

"They might just not want to go. You see, in many ways they're a very home loving couple, and I mean a couple. They do everything together and they live in a delightful village with two sets of adoring parents and have everything they want out of life within reach. They may be ambitious for themselves in the matter of their learning and physical development, but if you live in paradise, why leave it?" He spread out his hands on the table. "I expect though, that if their parents agree, they will probably gently persuade the girls that maybe it's time to broaden their horizons for a change." He paused thoughtfully.

"We can but try," he said. "I just hope we are not opening a can of worms that may destroy them eventually." He cast a bleak eye on the faces regarding him round the table. "We've wrecked a number of very good people's lives at one time or another," he finished bitterly.

"We've also saved a lot of other people's lives as well," he was reminded. So it was agreed that the girls would be approached through their parents, and if they agreed to the proposal a place would be found for them at a very elite institution which catered for specially gifted young ladies and here this chronicle must end. You may like to find out how they developed, their adventures and the challenges which they both faced when they finally enrolled at the Yvette Coleman Finishing School for Young Ladies in which they relate, in their own words and which have been faithfully collected and edited by your chronicler, the lives and happenings of these two exceptional young people.

Printed in Poland
by Amazon Fulfillment
Poland Sp. z o.o., Wrocław